DARK WOLF SOUL

MAFIA PACK #1

HEATHER HILDENBRAND

LEXI

*T*he last party remix of the night pumps through the club's speakers, seeping through the faded dressing room walls. After this, the music will switch to sexy slow dances until we close at two a.m. Gearing up for the night ahead of me, I look at myself in the dressing room mirror, taking in my appearance.

My white-blonde hair is still in its messy bun, and my green eyes are tired from working long hours. Some of those hours are paid, and some aren't. I spend way too much time at the teen shelter considering it's not helping me keep a roof over my head, but I can't help it. Those kids have no one, and I know what that's like firsthand. Besides, the exhaustion is nothing new. I've been on my own my whole life, which means I've never had the luxury of rest.

Although, the fact that every other girl working this place is making twenty times what I am is starting to wear on what I'd once thought was an iron-clad boundary.

Every other girl in this club comes here to dance for

cash plucked from the sticky, drunk fingers of anyone willing to pay to watch. Me? I managed to wedge my way into a job as a waitress at Shady Shags Dancing Palace— and nothing else. I have a feeling it's because Shady likes the idea of me being a big tease and using that to convince customers to part with their money in exchange for the girls who *are* willing to take their clothes off. I'm just glad that girl isn't me, although part of me knows, if I stay here long enough, someday it will be.

The truth is, my lease at the pay-weekly motel in Lakeland will end before I'll make enough to renew it. According to the notice they stuck beneath my door this morning, I have just under twenty-four hours left to catch up on back rent, and I know damn good and well I won't make a thousand dollars between now and then. Not waitressing anyway.

There are a number of things I *could* do. Lie. Steal. Cheat. Commit felonies. Or dance on the pole onstage for money. All of those things are on the other side of a line I told myself I would never cross. I'm not morally against stripping or even sex-work, but I have to claim control over something, and after growing up being tossed from home to home, autonomy over my body is the last remaining sense of power I have. Offering it up to strangers is a boundary I won't cross.

The problem is my boundaries won't mean shit when I'm homeless. Again.

I sigh, wondering for the millionth time how my life ended up like this. But it's a story as tired as I am of telling it. I never knew my family, and being an orphan has made my life difficult. Years spent in shitty group homes. Foster siblings who thought they had a right to my body and my belongings. Adults who took one look at me or my history and decided I was nothing but trouble.

Fuck the system; all it ever did was fail me.

I've been on my own my whole life and have always worked hard to make ends meet, but some lines can't be crossed. Mostly because you can't come back once you do. I'm grateful for this job, but it's not exactly the life I have in mind for myself.

Someday, I'm going to do something that matters. Something to make a difference in the lives of people who need it most.

"Lexi."

The sound of my name makes me jump. Through the mirror's reflection, I see Angel glaring at me. Her deep lines are more pronounced with the layers of makeup caked on top of her face—but don't tell her that unless you want to get laid out flat.

"Your shift starts in five, girl," she warns me. "Don't be late for the one thing you're actually good for around here."

I don't answer, which I know pisses her off, but I can't help myself. According to my friend, Violet, Angel's been here the longest of anyone. Ten years and still going. I have no idea how old she is, but she considers herself the mother hen of the roost, and she's meaner than a horny rooster if you cross her.

I don't play her power games, but I also don't start shit I don't want to finish.

Tonight, the only thing I want to finish is my shift. And maybe an extra-large burrito from Cantina. I fucking love burritos, and I don't give a shit if they go straight to my hips.

As I change into my uniform, a tight black mini-dress that shows off my curves, I mentally prepare myself for the night ahead. Serving drinks on the main floor is a bit unpredictable considering you never know what level of shitfaced the customers will be. But it's the VIP room clients that make me nervous, especially on weekends.

Today is Saturday, so I know exactly what to expect in the VIP room, and I'm not looking forward to it.

After stepping into my matching black heels, I take a second to put on some lipstick and mascara. It's the only makeup I bother with under the dim lighting, and even that is something I do for myself. Lipstick has always felt like a badge of courage, so I use what I've got at my disposal. The shade is called Death By Kisses, which seems like as good a way to go as any.

Finally, I pull my hair out of its messy bun and fluff it around my shoulders. The waves are a bit tangled, but I don't bother brushing them. The clients like that bedhead look, which means they'll tip better. Hopefully.

"Lexi, move your ass," Angel snaps.

"I'm going," I mutter, grabbing my purse and stuffing it into the cubby I share with Violet, the only dancer here I actually consider a friend.

As if I summoned her with my thoughts, Violet shows up just in time to snag my arm as I hurry out of the dressing room.

"Whoa, Speedy," she says with a smile.

Violet's always smiling—something I admire but find completely fucking batshit, considering the hard life she's lived in her twenty-four years. I'm only twenty-one, and I've already lost all fucking reason to summon any cheer.

"Hey," I say, noting the jar of glitter she's holding in one hand. Tonight is her trial run with a new routine where her naked body is covered in nothing but purple sparkles. Violet's creative that way. "Love the glitter choice."

"Thanks. I'm so excited," she gushes.

I shake my head.

"Break a leg, kid." I lightly punch her arm.

"Evan will break all their legs if anyone messes up the masterpiece."

Evan's our security guard, and while he's not a man of many words, he doesn't hesitate to put his fist through a face if the situation calls for it.

I snort. "I would pay to see that."

"Right? You want to do drinks after work?" she asks me. "My treat."

Normally, I'd say yes. Violet is a fun distraction with her sunny outlook and unending support. But I'm way too exhausted after spending the day trying to scrounge up extra cash for rent.

"I'm already yawning," I say. "Raincheck?"

"You're not sleeping enough again," she guesses.

"This time it's for a good cause," I assure her.

"That shelter asks too much of you," she says, which is a lecture I'm used to but also immune from.

"They don't have enough workers to keep up with the demand," I tell her. "You know how it is being alone on the street. Those kids deserve support."

She sighs. "That support can't always be from you."

I don't answer. My mind drifts to my own housing

issue looming and how I might very well be living at that shelter by the end of the week.

"Is everything okay?"

I blink and find her frowning as she studies my expression. Apparently, I suck at hiding my stress. It still feels strange to have someone else worry about me. It took me months to even trust that she was being real. Now that I do, I always get a lump in my throat and have to fight the urge to run away from it.

"It's fine," I tell her, refusing to put my problems on her. "I just need some extra cash, that's all."

The look in her eye says it all. But she won't say it out loud. She knows better than to suggest that I take the stage. "Let me know if there's anything I can do."

"You can get me good and drunk tomorrow after work," I tell her.

"It's a date. Now, I better run. This glitter isn't going to spread itself," she adds, wiggling her eyebrows at me.

"See you later," I call, chuckling as we go our separate ways.

The front of the club is already packed when I emerge. On stage, a nipple-tasseled Cleopatra grinds against the metal pole, eliciting cheers and an offer for her to be someone's queen for the night.

In other words, it's a normal night at Shady Shag's.

For the next few hours, I do my best to shut out the noise and focus on the work of serving drinks. Evan, the bouncer, watches the main floor like a hawk so anyone trying to get extra-handsy gets immediately tossed on their ass. I pretend it's out of some kind of concern for me, but the truth is Shady won't let anyone have a free ride. Now, if they've paid to be handsy—that's a different story.

But that only happens in the VIP room, anyway.

I manage to avoid serving anyone in the VIP area for almost the entire night.

It's not that I'm against naked lap dances or even consensual happy endings, although I still can't understand how Shady gets away with something so, well, shady. Either way, it's just not my jam to be the one giving those things in exchange for rent money, and I don't want to lose this job because some entitled frat guy got me mixed up with one of the dancers then ended up sucker-punched for his efforts.

I did that once during my first week here, and Shady said, if it ever happened again, I'd be out on my ass instead of the customer being out on his. Apparently, the only one allowed to punch someone is Evan. It's gender bias, I tell you.

At just after midnight, Reva, the bartender, waves me over. "Hey," she calls.

"What's this for?" I ask, nodding at the Old Fashioned she's shoving toward me.

"Tall, dark, and Big Dick Energy ordered it," she says.

I scan the tables, trying to figure out who she means. "Where?"

"VIP room," she says, and I tense.

"Not my area," I say, attempting to shove the drink back at her.

"You sure about that?" She arches a brow. "According to Violet, he asked for this drink and for you to deliver it."

"Me?"

7

"You're the only Lexi here."

Now, my guard is all the way up. Why bother asking for a waitress when they can have a dancer whose job it is to do a hell of a lot more than deliver a drink?

I consider refusing, but the drink taunts me. The tip I'll get on the other side of delivering it taunts me too.

Twenty-four hours.

A thousand dollars.

I have to stay focused.

"Whatever," I mutter, mostly to myself, and take the drink.

Weaving my way through tables, I make it to the VIP room with only two ass grabs for my trouble. Still, I'm grumpy and wary by the time I enter the VIP area.

The light is dimmer here with red bulbs tinting the black leather sofas, each sitting area separated by thin partitions. It's supposed to be sexy, but the smell of skin, sweat, and alcohol kind of ruins it for me. I guess if you're drunk enough, you don't notice.

The first seating area is occupied by a guy who looks barely old enough to get through the front door. Nevaeh grinds against him, her bare ass backed up to his chest. His hands are in places I know he's paying extra for, and I hurry past them before I have to make eye contact with anyone.

The second seating area is empty. The third couch has clothing strewn over it and an empty drink on the side table but no one in sight. I glance at the secret door that leads to a back room meant for more private encounters.

I keep walking into the fourth area. Empty. One more to go.

Violet exits the last section, and I tense. Her face lights up when she sees me. She's covered in nothing but bright purple glitter that I'm sure will take a heavy-handed scrub to wash off, and she's smiling in a way that has me suddenly wishing I'd refused this delivery.

"Someone's asking for you," she says as if it's my lucky day.

"Who is it?" I ask.

She shrugs. "No idea. He sat alone in the front of the house for an hour then moved back here fifteen minutes ago. He ordered that," she says, gesturing to the drink in my hand, "and you."

"What do you mean ordered me?"

She winks. "Take him the drink, and find out."

She starts to leave, but I stop her. "Vi, what do you mean *ordered*?"

She sighs. "He wants a private dance. But only from you."

"No way. I'm out of here." I shove the drink at her, but she doesn't take it.

"He offered a thousand dollars. Cash," she adds.

"That's between him and Shady—"

"He already paid the club for the spot. The thousand is your tip."

I stare at her. "Seriously?"

That's my rent money. What the fuck.

She studies me with a softening expression. "Look, I know you said you didn't want to dance, but... a thousand bucks buys a lot of burritos."

"Burritos aren't what I need," I mumble.

She softens. "I know."

9

Ugh.

"Look, just take him the drink, and see for yourself," she says gently. "If you don't like the vibe, walk away. It's your decision."

She's gone before I can think of a reason to argue with that logic.

I take a deep breath, squaring my shoulders. Fuck it. It's just an Old-Fashioned.

I turn and walk into the fourth and last VIP section.

The last sofa is empty.

I frown, unsure what to do, but then a looming shadow emerges from the darkened corner. Broad shoulders give way to the rest of him as he steps into the red-lit spotlight overhead. He's tall and well-dressed in a button-down shirt and suit slacks perfectly tailored to his form. I don't know a ton about fabric quality, but something tells me he doesn't shop at a box department store. The shirt sleeves have been rolled up to the elbow, revealing ink I can't quite make out in the dim lighting.

One thing I *can* see is that he's handsome as hell in a rugged, dangerous sort of way. The suit should have made him respectable-looking, but it only sends the message that this man has deep enough pockets to command whatever respect he doesn't earn.

His piercing blue eyes scan my body from head to toe in a lazy yet invasive inspection. Suddenly, the short dress I'm wearing doesn't seem like nearly enough to hide my vulnerable parts.

By the time his eyes reach mine again, I can't help but feel stripped bare already.

"You must be Lexi."

His deep voice scrapes along my skin, and I shudder at the intimate way he's touched me without lifting a finger.

What the hell, Lex? Get your shit together.

"You must be the Old-Fashioned." I hold the drink out, not bothering to step closer as I offer it.

He reaches over to take the drink from my hand. As he does, his fingers brush mine, and like some kind of traitor to the cause, my body literally tingles from our shared touch.

This is ridiculous.

Turning on my heel, I start to leave.

"You're not staying for the dance?"

I turn back, unable to stop the glare I give him. "I'm not a dancer."

"Well, I was thinking I'd be the judge of that."

His words are teasing, but his expression is more of a dare.

He reaches into his pocket and pulls out a wad of cash. "I'll make it worth your while."

I hesitate, eyeing the money and wondering if a roof over my head is worth it.

"How do you know my name?"

He takes a step forward. "The bartender mentioned it earlier."

The lie rolls off his tongue so easily I almost believe him.

"Who are you?"

He winks. "You can call me Old Fashioned."

Expensive suit. No name. Alarm bells go off in my mind.

"I'm only a waitress," I say, taking a step back.

"Not for the next ten minutes."

I roll my eyes. Clearly, he thinks he's charming.

But sexy and charming are two different things.

Not that I think he's sexy.

Or not that I care.

"You're willing to pay a lot for a dance from someone who's never done it before."

"Is one thousand a lot?"

Prick.

"It's a very specific number," I tell him.

"Is it the right number for you to say yes?"

His eyes spark with the dare, and I can feel myself getting just angry enough to prove... whatever I'm trying to prove.

Fuck it.

"Sit down and keep your hands to yourself," I say before I can talk myself out of it.

His grin is sly, and the urge to sucker-punch it off his sexy face is strong. Instead, I keep my eyes on the prize in his hand.

The cash.

He tosses it onto the small side table beside his untouched drink and then settles himself on the couch before looking up at me expectantly.

As if on cue, the song coming from the speakers overhead changes to something slow and sultry.

Before I can talk myself out of it, I shove my hands into my hair and begin to dance for him. He watches me like I'm something to eat, and despite the fact that I told myself I'd never do this, I can't help but wonder what it would be like to let him feast on me.

My pulse races at the thought.

There's a hidden door in every single section of the VIP area, including this one, but I don't dare let myself glance at it. Something tells me he knows about it already anyway. And I refuse to cross that line too, no matter how sexy this stranger is.

His eyes remain on me the entire time, but he follows my instructions about keeping his hands to himself. He's not like the other men I've witnessed in here. He's actually respecting my boundaries.

Maybe that's what makes me braver.

As the song builds, I climb onto his lap and straddle him. My dress hikes up on my thighs as I lower myself to his hips. Grinding against him, I watch as his gaze darkens with a desire that borders on dangerous.

Somewhere in the back of my mind, I order myself to stop this insanity, but whatever reason or common sense I'd clung to earlier is gone. Now that I'm touching him, I can't seem to make myself stop.

I shudder at the way he watches me with hooded eyes, and without meaning to, I dip lower. My movements feel more like foreplay than a dance. This time, when I thrust against him, I feel his erection rub my thigh.

The feel of it startles me, but more than that, it turns me on.

My skin heats, and my core aches for more.

Still, he doesn't touch me, and I have to press my lips together to keep from asking him to. Forcing myself to ease up just a little, I put some distance between me and his dick before I can do something stupid. Like try to sit on it. Without the barrier of clothing between us.

Apparently, he's not the only one whose blue balls I need to worry about here.

But even with the space between us, I can feel the heat coming off of him too. I don't need his hands on me to know he wants this. Me. Desire laces the air between us until I can barely breathe without choking on it. His. Mine. It's all the same.

I've never been this turned on in my life.

When the song ends, a new one starts, but I go still, staring back at him with enough tension between us to cut with a knife.

Slowly, he sits forward and reaches around me. I hold my breath, fully expecting him to finally break my rule and touch me. My skin tingles at the mere thought, and I know, if he does, I'll give in to whatever he wants—including the back room.

Instead, he grabs the cash off the side table and holds it out to me.

As he leans back again, he whispers in my ear, "You're beautiful, Lexi. Absolutely stunning."

I blush at his words, feeling a strange connection to him. But before I can say anything, he holds up the money and adds, "Thank you for the dance."

The dance.

Right.

This is just a transaction.

Shit.

I scramble to my feet, nearly tripping as my shoe threatens to buckle sideways. Managing to remain upright, I shove my dress down my thighs and shake my head, trying to clear my thoughts.

"Thanks," I mumble, snatching the cash out of his hand and nearly sprinting away from him.

He's just another customer, I remind myself.

Except, I'm pretty sure I'll never be the same again after that dance.

2

GREY

I must have lost my damned mind. Asking the mark for a lap dance? That's not part of the plan, and yet, once the idea came to me, I couldn't resist the temptation. Sitting here now with her draped over my thighs, her hair falling around us like a curtain, is worth every rule I've just broken for myself. After two days of watching her from afar, I have to admit she's even more breathtaking up close. All that long, thick hair just asking to be taken by the fistful, and those sharp green eyes practically begging me to break the only rule she gave me for this little performance.

All I want is my hands on her.

Lie.

I want more than my hands on her.

I want my cock inside her.

Unfortunately for me, that's nowhere near what I've come here tonight to do. Which means the no-touching rule is one I won't let myself break. Not because I respect her wishes but because there's something about her that calls to me—and I can't afford this girl's siren song getting into my blood.

Already, I've gotten closer than I should. Maybe it's those lonely eyes. The way they seem to ask for something without her having to say a word. Or maybe I've gone soft in my old age. Twenty-seven years is hardly ancient, but it feels like a century since I let a woman touch me like she's doing. I've spent years honing my control, learning how to read a threat, and staying the hell away from anything that can get me killed.

Lexi triggers all three, yet here I sit, hard as granite and wishing I didn't have to stop at a lap dance. It's been a long damn time since any woman stirred me this way, but none have ever made me stray from the plan like this.

Her hips undulate as she rocks against me, and I swallow back a groan. When she grinds against my erection, I nearly lose it. Instead, I fist my hands and grind my teeth to remain still. Years of training and it's all led me to a moment where my control is hanging by a thread.

It would be so easy to rip her panties off and sheath myself inside her. I bet she's wet already. The scent of her arousal is a drug threatening to suck me into its spell.

Finally, the song ends, which is both a relief and a disappointment. She goes still, sitting on my lap and staring at me with an open invitation in her gorgeous green eyes.

She wants me to keep going.

If she were anyone else, I'd do it too.

But she's not anyone else, and very soon, she's going to hate me. In this moment, I'm the only one of us who knows it, just like I know she'll hate herself along with me if I don't stop now. So, instead of peeling this excuse of a dress off her thighs and burying myself inside her right here, I reach around and grab the cash I promised her. The cash I knew would be too tempting to resist.

I'm an asshole, but I've made my peace with it.

Mostly.

"You're beautiful, Lexi," I tell her before offering her the money. "Absolutely stunning."

She looks like she might just close the deal herself, so I remind her what this is. What it has to be. "Thank you for the dance."

Her expression shutters, and she scrambles off me, turning away but not before I see her cheeks flush in embarrassment. She's ashamed of herself for thinking this was more than a business exchange. And I'm ashamed of myself for letting her think it isn't.

Dammit.

"Thank you," she mumbles, snatching the money from my hand and then practically running out of the room.

When she's gone, I let my head fall back on the couch and close my eyes, breathing through the ache in my balls. My erection pulses against my pants, and my wolf snarls at me for letting her go.

It's his involvement that made me do it, though, so he can suck it.

Lexi Giovanni is, for all intents and purposes, my greatest enemy, but apparently, no one told that to the beast that lives inside me—or my hard-as-steel cock. And both of them have no problem letting me know I'm outnumbered.

Straightening, I reach for the drink and gulp it down.

The alcohol burns just enough to clear my head and calm my twitching dick.

When I'm pretty sure I can walk without a limp, I shove to my feet and let myself out through the back door so I can get my shit together before the next phase begins. Unfortunately for Lexi, I'm nowhere near done with her yet, and I have a feeling she's not going to find this next part nearly as thrilling as she did the first. I tell myself I won't like it either, but my wolf's anticipation is unmistakable.

Get your shit together, man.

She's just a mark.

One last debt to pay. All I have to do is deliver her straight to hell and trade her freedom for my own.

3

LEXI

By the time I collect myself and re-emerge from the staff bathroom, the stranger is gone. His disappearance leaves me feeling strangely abandoned. It's stupid. I mean, what did I want? For him to fall under the spell of my gyrating hips and profess his undying obsession with my body? Ugh. Sure, a girl has needs, but never seeing him again is safer. Because if he ever comes back, looking for an encore, I'm not sure I'll have it in me to refuse him the full service.

Three hours later, I'm sticky and smelly and trying like hell not to overthink the boundary I've crossed with myself tonight. Evan follows the last customer to the door then manhandles him through it since the guy doesn't want to leave without "his queen by his side."

As the other girls gather over drinks at the bar, Violet high-fives me, which I know is her attempt at lightening my mood, but all it does is make the other girls ask what happened. The moment they hear I gave a private dance, their glances become knowing.

"It's only a matter of time now," Cleopatra says with a smirk. "Once you start making that kind of cash, it's impossible to go back."

I don't answer her, but I catch Angel watching me, and the hard look she wears makes me shudder. Before she can say anything, I duck my head and go back to wiping tables with renewed enthusiasm.

One by one, the dancers disappear into the back room to change and then head out for the night. Violet offers to hang, but I turn her down again. My exhaustion is even more pronounced after my crazy-ass evening.

Violet promises drinks tomorrow instead and then leaves. Reva, the bartender, follows suit. Shady is hunkered down in his office, counting the night's cash, leaving only Evan and me to finish up out front.

A few minutes later, Evan waves at me as he heads out.

"You want me to stay and walk you?" he asks.

"Nah, I'll be fine."

"You sure?"

"I'm sure. Shady's still here," I tell him, waving him on.

Besides, I could use some quiet after the chaos of the past few hours.

He leaves, and I hurry to finish my work. When the last table has been cleaned and all of the chairs have been stacked, I turn in my apron and head for the staff exit in back.

At the door, I hesitate, wondering if I should ask Shady to escort me out. It's a rule for the dancers that they can't leave alone—for safety. But I'm not a dancer, and I've never heard of an obsessed customer stalking the waitress. Besides, Shady is on my list of people to avoid, especially since he would have heard about my VIP show by now and undoubtedly plans to use it as an excuse to offer me a promotion.

Again.

With that in mind, I slip outside and head for my car. The two-door beater was a gift from the shelter for my volunteer work. It's lasted three years so far, which, according to Violet, is three years past its expiration date. Now, the heap of metal is probably one pothole away from disintegrating, but I try not to think too hard about future problems considering my current ones are bad enough. Living in it will suck, but I try not to think about that either. Maybe this time, I'll leave the tiny town of Lakeland, North Carolina behind, start over somewhere new.

Lost in worry, I don't register just how quiet it is in the gravel lot until I'm halfway across it and the hairs on the back of my neck stand on end. Suddenly, all I notice *is* the silence.

A sense of being watched has me glancing back. There's no one there.

I force myself to breathe and keep walking.

The wind lifts my hair, sending the ends of it dancing in a breeze that might have felt refreshing—if it didn't also bring a sense of foreboding.

The club is on the edge of town, which means no traffic comes through unless they're headed straight here. The isolation has never bothered me before, but suddenly, it leaves me feeling exposed. Vulnerable.

Two things I hate feeling.

The sensation of being watched grows stronger.

I glance around again, peering into the thick trees that

border the employee parking lot, but there's nothing visible in the darkness that wraps the night. The only car left in the lot besides mine is Shady's lifted truck.

No one else is here, I tell myself.

If there was another car, even out on the street, I'd see it from here.

From behind Shady's truck, a noise sounds, and I freeze.

In the stillness, a creature steps into sight.

I stare in shock as a wolf, larger than anything I've ever seen, stares back at me. Its fur is dark, but its eyes glow bright yellow—and they're narrowed on me.

I force myself to take a shallow breath and whisper, "Easy, boy."

Wolves aren't unheard of in the hills surrounding our tiny rural town, but they don't come this close or show aggression toward humans for no reason.

At my words, the wolf bares its teeth and emits a low growl.

It takes a step toward me, and panic erases all thoughts in my mind. Before I can decide if it's smart, I turn and run. My bag falls out of my hand, but I don't bother going back for it. The gravel is uneven, and my feet wobble beneath me as I aim for the club door. Somehow, the wolf manages to cut me off, blurring past me and planting itself between me and the staff entrance.

I pull up short.

The wolf looks back at me with an awareness that feels impossible. But I can't deny it just anticipated my route and blocked it rather than coming straight at me.

What the actual fuck?

Why would it do that?

How is it even possible?

Not waiting to find out, I spin around and sprint for the woods. The moment I reach the tree line, I know I'm fucked. The wolf is too fast, already on my heels as I zig-zag through the maze of trees. Low branches smack me in the face and scrape along my bare arms, but I ignore them, focusing only on finding a tree with a branch low enough for me to grab. I took rock-wall climbing at the rec center during a free summer camp for foster kids once, and now it's the only hope I have of escape.

I refuse to be one of those bimbo bitches who trips while running from the monster and gets killed before the opening credits are done.

But that's fiction, and this is real life.

And in real life, wolves are fast as shit.

He's on me in no time.

I don't fall, but I recognize my mistake way too late. Just ahead, a large rock formation rises in front of me like a wall. I try to veer left but the wolf nips at my heels, sending me straight ahead. I do the same move to the right and get a scrape of teeth along my calf for my trouble.

Shit.

I hit the wall with both palms, nearly slamming my face into it, thanks to my momentum. Then I whirl, my back pressed to the wall, and try to prepare myself to be eaten alive.

But the wolf only stands several yards away, watching me with those orb eyes that hold more awareness than they should.

"Just get it over with already," I snap.

Apparently, near-death experiences make me cranky.

Instead, the wolf shudders, and I hear a pop as its bones begin to crack.

What the fuck.

Right before my eyes, the wolf transforms.

One second, it's a creature with four legs and fur. The next, it's a man.

A very naked man.

"What...?"

I can't help but scan his bared body. Broad shoulders, a muscular chest decorated with a swirling black tattoo, ripped abs that make it, frankly, unfair for the rest of the male population. And that perfectly shaped V pointing like an arrow straight to the largest dick I've ever seen.

The fact that it isn't even at full mast is honestly impressive—even in my current state of questioning everything I think I know about the world.

But it's his face that sends me reeling more than anything else.

I know that face.

I just saw it close-up earlier tonight.

The handsome stranger I lap-danced for mere hours ago stands before me now on full display—and he's somehow capable of becoming a giant wolf.

Shock and panic overwhelm me, and I can feel my head spinning as everything I thought was true about being human is shattered.

"You are... that was... how is this possible?"

"How is what possible?" he demands.

"You were... a wolf."

His eyes narrow. "Don't play stupid; it's annoying."

"Excuse me?"

"And don't make this harder than it has to be."

"Make what harder? Letting you kill me?"

"You're coming with me," he says in a voice that sounds nothing like the teasing, sexy version of him I met earlier.

Now, there is only danger, and it's not the kind that turns me on, either.

"Coming with you where?" I ask, trying to understand what he wants from me.

"Your time in hiding is up. Don't make me take you by force."

The stranger takes a step toward me, and the sight of him approaching sends me over the edge. The world tilts then spins, and my knees buckle. My eyes flutter, and I gasp for air, trying like hell to keep my wits about me. But the sight of him approaching, and the grim look he gives me, tells me this isn't going to end well at all. As he reaches out for me, black spots creep into my vision. Then, all at once, darkness swallows me whole.

4

GREY

She shouldn't have run. That's what I tell myself as I carry her unconscious body to the car I've hidden down the road. If she hadn't run, I wouldn't have chased her. And she might not have passed out from the shock of watching my wolf nearly mow her down. Then again, any normal she-wolf would have known running was the most dangerous thing she could have done with a beast like me at her heels. More than that, any normal she-wolf dumb enough to run would have at least shifted to capitalize on the extra speed her wolf would offer. There's no way she could ever outrun me on foot.

But Lexi didn't shift, and even now, I can't scent her wolf on her at all.

It's like she's nothing more than human.

If I hadn't been nearly skin-to-skin with her earlier and felt the powerful animal inside her, I would be wondering if I'd gotten the wrong girl. But even through my own lust back at that club, I'd sensed her wolf buried deep. There was no mistaking her nature then. Even if I can't sense it now.

It's just another mystery to solve, not that it matters for what we have planned for her. Hell, if she never shifts, it'll probably make things easier on her. Not that I have any right to care what's easier for her considering I'm locking her in a trunk and driving off with her.

She doesn't stir as I gently deposit her into the trunk of the car I chose for this mission. It's the least flashy option compared to the others my father apparently kept stored for me all these years, but it also has the roomiest trunk. Her small frame fills the entire space, and I frown, knowing she's going to be cramped when she wakes.

With the lid still open, I press my fingers to her throat, checking to make sure her pulse is still strong and her breathing is still regular. Her skin is soft beneath mine, and I can't help thinking what it would be like to run my hands over it as she straddles me, grinding against me, all that hair draping us like a curtain. Satisfied her vitals are good, I go to work binding her wrists and feet. She's unlikely to free herself from the trunk, but I've learned over the years to never assume Plan A will work.

When I'm finished, I catch myself studying her mouth like it's some sort of eighth world wonder. Her bottom lip is slightly fuller than the top. I have no idea why that's so enticing.

Fuck.

I do not need this kind of distraction.

Yanking my gaze away, I step back and close the trunk, rounding the front of the car.

There's a change of clothes on the passenger seat, so I

put them on quickly and then slide behind the wheel. The suit is no real loss. In fact, it's one of the things I was more than happy to leave behind when I left this life. Now that I'm back in it, the wardrobe requirements are as stifling as they've always been. My father always did care more about perception than reality. For now, I wear the black pants and matching t-shirt that have become my uniform since I've been away.

Grabbing the keys from where I stashed them in the visor, I start the car. The night is silent around me, so the engine coming to life sounds louder than it should, but my wolf senses tell me there's no one around to hear it.

I check my phone. Three messages, all from him.

Ignoring them, I put the car into gear and ease onto the road, keeping my headlights off as I pass the club on my way to the main highway up ahead. The two cars from earlier remain in the lot. One is hers. If it mattered, I could move her car somewhere they'd never find it. Give myself a bigger lead on getting her far away. But I don't need it. They'll never find her where I'm taking her, and there's not really anyone to look anyway.

I watched her for two days, which was more than enough time to realize she's pretty much alone in the world. Behind on her rent, one friend she keeps at a distance, and all her free time spent at a homeless shelter for runaway teens. If she weren't my enemy, I'd feel sorry for her shitty circumstances. Regardless of her family name, she deserved a hell of a lot more than Franco Giovanni ever gave her. But that's not my problem, nor is it my business.

My phone vibrates with an incoming call, and since I

already know he won't stop until I answer, I hit the button to accept.

"Yeah," I say quietly as the call goes live on the car's Bluetooth.

"How'd it go?"

"I got her," I say.

He exhales in relief. It's clear he doubted I'd come through. I don't take it personally. My father doubts everyone except himself, a trait he apparently passed on to me.

"Don't act so surprised," I say mostly to rile him.

"How far out are you?" he asks.

"A few hours. I'll text you when we get close."

"Is she subdued?"

"She's out," I confirm. I don't tell him she passed out from shock rather than the drugs he supplied.

"Good. Call me if there are any issues."

"There won't be."

He grumbles at that, but I disconnect the call before he can keep going. Next thing, he'll ask me to alert him every time I piss or breathe. Not for the first time since being summoned home, my chest aches with the sense of entrapment. My father expects me to pick up right where I left off—well, that and to act like he's saved me from some horrible fate by forcing me back home. The asshole can't imagine any life better than the one he's provided me.

I don't need to imagine. For the last few years, I lived it. A life where I didn't answer to a cruel monster who cares only for himself and nothing for the people he hurts. A life where I got to decide what and who to fight for. For five years, I finally had my freedom. And the moment this mission is over, I plan to go right back to it again.

The highway traffic is light, thanks to the late hour. I opt for silence instead of music as my tires eat up the road. It's almost peaceful out here—if you don't count the felony I just committed or the war waiting for me back home.

Maybe my father's right to be surprised I came through for him. I damn sure didn't want to. But I'll never be free of him if I keep running, which I can admit is what I've been doing for years. It's time to stop running and face what I am. What I'm supposed to become. Even if it means doing something like this to someone like her.

My phone vibrates again, but this time when I see the caller, I answer it without the pit in my stomach.

"Dutch, what's up?" I say.

"How'd it go, brother?"

"Fine. I'm on my way back now."

"No hiccups."

"Easy day," I assure him.

"The old man must be pleased as punch."

"He's shocked I'm capable," I say, and he chuckles darkly.

"I'll bet. You're bringing home the Ace this family's needed in their hand."

"She's not a poker chip, Dutch. She's a fucking person."

He's silent for a beat before he asks pointedly, "And is this person attractive?"

"Fuck you," I grumble, and he chuckles, unbothered by my response.

"What? I saw the picture the old man gave you."

"That was taken two years ago, wise-ass."

"That's why I'm asking for a status update."

"Is there something else you needed?" I ask, though I know full well he's not going to stop giving me a hard time about this. Dutch is my second cousin on my mom's side, but he's more like a brother at this point. He'd do anything for me—even help me leave the family in the dead of night so that I couldn't be tracked down again for four full years.

My dad will never forgive him for helping me, which means his career in this family is fucked unless I come back to stay and help him move up the ranks again, which is the last thing I want to do. He doesn't seem to care, though. Dutch is solid like that.

In fact, he's already made it clear he's loyal to me, no matter what my old man thinks. Starting with the fact that he's reporting to me directly instead of my father with every order he's been given since I stepped foot back inside the borders of Indigo Hills.

"We found the guy I told you about. The one feeding Franco intel."

Apparently, Dutch discovered a rat a few weeks ago. He took it to my father first, but the old man's too cocky to worry about someone being able to get to him and told Dutch not to worry about it. So, Dutch came to me, and I gave him the green light to investigate. My father's big head's going to be his downfall if he's not careful because, apparently, Dutch was right all along.

"That was fast," I say.

"It's the only thing I'm fast at, don't worry."

I shake my head. "You got a name?"

"Trucker."

"That piece of shit," I snarl.

32

"You remember him?"

"How could I forget? He's one of our oldest captains. Asshole's always been a bit big for his panties. Thinks he should be running shit instead of my old man."

The prick also didn't like to take no for an answer when it came to the ladies, which deserved an ass-kicking far worse than ever betraying the boss did if you asked me.

"What do you want me to do?" Dutch asks, grunting his agreement of my assessment.

"Bring him in," I say. "See if you can find out if we have any other rats on our end."

"You don't think he's working alone?" Dutch asks.

I snort. "He's not smart enough for that."

"You got it. I'll call when we have more."

"Thanks, Dutch."

"Don't mention it. Listen, I know it's not what you wanted, but I'm glad you're back. We've missed you around here."

"I missed you too, man." That part, at least, isn't a lie.

"Aww." He pretends to sniffle, and I grin. "Okay, that's enough sappy shit," he declares. "I'll check in soon."

I shake my head.

"Later," I say as the call ends.

In the silence that follows, my thoughts drift from Trucker to Franco and then back to my father and his master plan that sent me out here in the first place. Lexi Giovanni, the long-lost princess, now a bargaining chip in the biggest bid for power the mafia pack has seen since its inception.

I still can't believe Franco's heir has been shaking her

tits at a strip club. No, not shaking them, I realize. Not until tonight. Not for anyone but me.

At first, I'd thought her friend was just saying that to flatter me. To make my tip bigger. But one look at Lexi's hesitation and I knew it was true. I was her first.

Just the memory of her on my lap makes me hard all over again.

I shake it off, trying like hell to forget, but it's impossible. It's not just her hot-as-sin body or the way she moved it against mine. Despite how badly she needed that money I offered her, she hadn't been afraid to tell me to go to hell. In fact, even though she'd given in and danced for me, and even though I knew she wanted me as badly as I wanted her, something about the way she looked at me made it clear she was still in charge of herself. That her boundaries meant more than her desires. Damn if I don't respect the hell out of that.

Lexi isn't what I expected at all.

Then again, I'm sure I'm not what she thought either. Or I won't be, once she wakes up and realizes what I've done. The idea of her hating me bothers me more than it should, and I grip the wheel tighter as I let the inevitable play out in my mind. Her waking up, finding out who I am, what I intend to do with her.

Dammit.

I might have taken her to make her a pawn in my father's war, but one night in her company and I know she's so much more than that. She doesn't deserve what's going to happen next. And even though it makes me an asshole of the worst kind, I'm doing nothing to stop it.

5

LEXI

I come awake slowly, some part of my brain convinced I'm hungover. It makes sense at first. My muscles are tight, my joints stiff, and my thoughts are hazy. But the moment I open my eyes and see the strangeness of my surroundings, I know alcohol has nothing to do with this nightmare.

The space I'm in is small and confining, the air thick and musty. Beneath whatever box I'm trapped inside, I sense movement. The kind of speed that comes from four wheels. A car.

Shit. That means I'm in a trunk.

I open my mouth, ready to scream for help when common sense prevails. If we're moving, that means whoever's driving is not interested in helping me. In fact, it's the opposite.

Whoever's driving is taking me.

I need to be smart.

My thoughts shift to how I ended up here. The last thing I remember is being chased by a wild wolf. No, wait.

The last thing I remember is watching that wolf shift into a man. A naked, muscled, chiseled, hot-as-sin man whose erection I teased only hours prior.

It's like something straight out of Twilight—if Twilight had taken place at a strip club and the wolf pack had been well-dressed kidnappers.

But werewolves can't possibly exist. This is *real life*.

Ugh.

Except that I know what I saw. And the reality of such an impossibility makes my head swim—which is exactly the kind of pansy-ass reaction that landed me caught in the first place. I can't afford that shit again.

Forcing myself to remain calm, I inspect the tiny space I'm curled inside. My wrists and ankles are bound with heavy cord, which explains the tight muscles and stiff joints, but I do my best to feel around for some kind of way out. I read somewhere once that all trunks have an emergency release button inside them, but after a full exploration of the space, I find nothing even close.

Fear threatens to send me spiraling as I force myself to look for another option. Running my hands along the wall, I find a small gap. Shoving my fingers through, I realize it's an opening between the back seats. Not that getting into the car with my kidnapper is a great plan, but it's the only one that gets me out of the trunk, and I can't just do nothing.

Shoving as hard as I can against it yields no movement.

Determined, I twist and contort my body, moving around so I can position my feet against the seat back. Using all my strength, I kick at the seat with both feet and am rewarded when the seat finally collapses forward.

Without wasting a second of the element of surprise, I hurl myself through the opening and into the backseat of the car.

Through the rearview mirror, my eyes meet those of my kidnapper. He registers only a hint of surprise and then veers off the road so suddenly that I'm tossed sideways against the door. Grunting from the impact, I struggle to right myself and twist so I can reach for the door handle. But he slams on the brakes, sending me faceplanting against the back of the driver's seat. Pain explodes along my cheekbone, and I jerk upright again, pissed off as well as terrified.

He climbs out of the car and wrenches open my door, his stormy eyes narrowed and full of threats.

"Get away from me." I shrink away from him, but he snags my wrists and yanks them toward him. With his other hand, he produces a sharp blade.

I struggle harder.

"Stop fucking moving."

Despite my fear, the sound of his voice sends a shudder through me that's more pleasure than panic.

I shake the thought off.

What the fuck, Lexi. He's a kidnapper.

He reaches out and cuts the bindings on my ankles then does the same to my wrists.

I cradle my hands, rubbing at my sore wrists and studying him with mixed feelings. Cutting me loose is a good thing... unless it's only going to lead to worse things.

"Don't fucking try to escape," he warns.

"Or what? You'll drug me again?"

"I didn't drug you," he says, and I'm about to argue when he adds, "yet."

Behind him, night has cloaked the lonely highway in complete darkness. There's not a single other car in sight. Far in the distance, a shadow of mountains looms, and I try to figure out where I am, but it's not enough to go on. Lakeland is already smack dab in the center of the Blue Ridge Mountains, and we clearly haven't left the area entirely.

"Do you promise to behave if I let you ride up front?"

I don't answer.

He straightens and steps back, letting me climb out of the backseat.

The moment my feet hit the gravel shoulder, I start running.

Unfortunately, my bare feet are no match for the sharp rocks, and my run turns instantly to a pained limp.

He catches me immediately, wrapping one strong arm around my waist and lifting me clear off my feet like I weigh nothing at all.

I open my mouth to scream, but he covers it with his other hand. I breathe in the scent of his skin, hating how much I like it. My body reacts like the traitor she is as the memory of being this close to him earlier tonight slams into me. How much I'd wanted to give him more than a lap dance.

Now, he's going to take whatever he wants, whether I give it or not.

Backtracking to the still-open car door, he sets me on my feet but keeps his arm wrapped firmly around me. His hand releases my mouth, and I suck in a breath before screaming again.

"Help!"

Something sharp pricks my neck, the unexpected pain cutting off my scream. A second later, the pain is gone, and the stranger is tucking something away then adjusting his grip on me.

"What the hell was that?" I demand.

"Relax. It's not going to hurt you."

"Liar."

The hand around my waist spins me so that I come face to face with my captor, my back against the open car doorframe.

In the darkness, I look up into a pair of glacier blue eyes that are filled with fury as they glare down at me. His full mouth is downturned into a frown that borders on a snarl, and my heart races at all the things he's probably going to do to me now.

"I have a sexually transmitted infection," I blurt, fear making me babble on. "You don't want to touch me. You'll get a rash, and it's gross, and you'll be sorry and—"

"Whoa. Geezus, relax. I'm not going to do anything like that."

"You're not?"

"No."

"Then what…"

Whatever drug he stuck me with kicks in. My limbs suddenly feel like they weigh a ton. My knees buckle, but his arms come around me and keep me from crumpling. His movements are sure and quick as he tosses me into the car. He leans inside, reaching for the seat belt. While he's distracted, I manage to land a solid punch to his jaw that has him cursing and backing off a little.

"You hit me." He looks more stunned than angry.

"What the fuck else do you expect, asshole?" I glare at him. "You can't kidnap a girl and expect her to go along willingly."

He bites off his response, shaking his head irritably. "Fine, you want to escape, be my fucking guest, but we're in Indigo Hills now, and if anyone else finds you out here, I can promise they won't be as nice as me."

He straightens, holding the car door open wide.

I launch myself out the open door but immediately fall to my knees as the drugs he gave me paralyze my limbs. Even climbing to my feet proves impossible, so I lie there, cussing and calling him every name I can think of. Which is a lot.

He stands over me, staring down at where I lie on the gravel. "You have a colorful vocabulary."

The amusement in his voice threatens to send me over the edge.

"You think this is funny?" I demand. "This is my fucking life you're messing with. I will kill you for this."

"I'm sure you want to," he says. "But I don't think that's an option for you at the moment."

"Fuck you."

"Contrary to what you think, I'll pass."

I respond by letting out an ear-splitting scream. It echoes against the silence of the night, but there's no response. No one else out here to come save me.

I know that because, instead of looking worried at the noise, the asshole groans, and a second later, he wraps an arm around my waist and picks me up off the ground, shoving me back inside the car.

"You said I could go," I protest, wiggling against him, which is, apparently, all I'm capable of at this point.

"I was making a point," he growls.

The snarl he makes as he wrestles me into place reminds me of before when I'd watched him literally change from a wolf to a man. My stomach drops, and I stop wriggling just as he leans across me and straps the seatbelt across my body.

"Do I have to duct tape you to the seat?"

"What are you?" I can't help but ask.

"What?"

"I saw you. You were a wolf. Then you turned into… this." I glance at his body, which is now clothed in a pair of black pants and a matching tee that hugs his biceps in ways I wish I didn't notice.

"You're incredibly observant," he says dryly, but the way he's watching me suggests he's testing me somehow. I pretend not to notice our sudden closeness and remind myself he's a kidnapper.

"Don't patronize me, asshole. And let me go."

His brow arches. "Or what?"

"Or my boyfriend and his gang will make you wish you'd never laid eyes on me."

"You're not a very good liar. You should work on that."

He reaches into the car along the sideboard and produces a roll of actual duct tape. I stare at him—and it—with wide eyes.

"What the hell are you going to do with that?"

"Look, despite what you think right now, I'm the safest

person in this fucking town for you. And since your self-preservation is at a negative number tonight, I'm going to help you live through this experience."

He makes a show of unwrapping the duct tape and then reaches in and presses the ends of it to the leather seat—with me strapped between.

"Oh, hell no," I say.

Fighting him is useless. My limbs are still unresponsive. He's easily able to hold me down and tape me to the seat. When he's finished, he tosses the duct tape onto the floorboard and shuts the car door.

A second later, he slides back into the driver's seat and puts the car into gear. We ease onto the highway, headed to whatever destination he's decided on. And I know with startling clarity that, whatever happens next, I'm completely at his mercy now.

42

6

GREY

*H*er shock over my wolf is real, I'm sure of it. Not only because her comment about a boyfriend earlier was so clearly a lie—a terrible one at that. But not even my wolf can sense a manipulation in her words, and he's got a gift for that sort of thing, which means this girl really doesn't know shifters exist. And the only way she can be oblivious to that is if she's never shifted herself. It's nearly impossible to think about, but there's no other answer. Not impossible, I remember, thinking of the other shifters I've heard about recently whose wolves were blocked.

Ash Lawson, co-alpha of the Lone Wolf pack, didn't shift for the first time until she was almost Lexi's age. I don't know the details or how they muted her wolf for so long, but at least I know it's possible. Unfortunately, Lexi clearly isn't ready to know it too. Not while she's convinced I'm going to force myself on her.

I grip the wheel with white-knuckled frustration.

This was supposed to be a simple snatch-and-grab

mission, and instead, I'm all twisted up about what my prisoner thinks of me.

Fuck.

It shouldn't matter.

But it does.

And it's about to get a whole lot worse. For both of us.

7

LEXI

*T*hanks to whatever drug I've been injected with and the duct tape strapping me to the seat, my mouth is the only thing that still functions, so, as we drive, I use it.

"Where the hell are you taking me?" I demand, pretending fear isn't gnawing a hole in my insides.

No answer. Not even a flick of a glance in my direction.

"What are you going to do with me?"

Still nothing.

My temper flares. "You won't get away with this."

The asshole doesn't so much as sniff in my direction, and I have to fight the urge to scream. His silence is impressive—or it would be if it weren't infuriating.

The longer we drive, the more nervous I become. He wasn't wrong. All the signs we pass are for places in Indigo Hills, a town I've only ever heard to stay out of. According to the rumors in Lakeland, it's run by the mafia, which I used to think was just a hilarious thing to say at parties.

What kind of mafia hid out in the mountains of North Carolina? But Violet's brother once took a loan from a guy from Indigo Hills. When he failed to pay it back, he vanished, and no one ever found him.

That's all I know, and it's more than enough to keep me far away from its borders until now. A single girl with no support or protection is a prime target for assholes—as evidenced by my current predicament.

By the time we finally reach the city, dawn has broken, sending innocent pink streaks across the softening blue sky.

The sun is just beginning to rise behind us, though I can't quite twist that far around to see it.

"What's in Indigo Hills?"

Still nothing.

I huff.

"Can you at least tell me your name?"

More silence.

"For fuck's sake, you already know mine. And what harm will it do when you have me duct taped to a car seat?"

His eyes flick to mine in the rearview. "Grey."

The fact that he answered startles me, but I shove past it quickly, hoping for more.

"Grey what?"

He shakes his head and averts his dark gaze back to the road.

The barren highway gives way to a few houses and businesses. Then, minutes later, we're swallowed up by a huge city. I stare out the windows, taken aback by the teeming metropolis.

"What is this place?" I ask, gaping at the urban landscape.

"Indigo Hills."

"No shit. I mean, how is it so huge?"

He snorts, and my cheeks heat at the innuendo I've just uttered. My mind flashes with images I shouldn't care about. Like how huge my tall, dark, and dickhead of a kidnapper is…in places.

Pretending I'm not picturing him naked, I stare up at the skyscrapers blotting out the early-morning sky. Around us, the city has already come to life. Or maybe it never slept. Traffic clogs the streets. Pedestrians dart between bumpers. Horns signal road rage. Instead of being the only car on the road, we're one in a sea of hundreds, which makes me invisible in a completely different way than before.

On the sidewalk, cart owners peddle breakfast items or newspapers and magazines. I try to catch their eye, but the tinted windows make it impossible. No one knows I'm back here, and even if they did, all they'd see is a girl sitting still in the backseat of a sedan.

Damn this stupid duct tape.

Damn Grey to hell.

We drive past the taller buildings, turning right once and then left. The offices become condos and apartments. They look expensive with their perfect landscaping and concrete fountains. I try to track our route, but it's impossible when the city is so huge and foreign to me.

We make a left into a parking lot with valet parking attendants, and my heart leaps with hope. But he only

47

waves at them through his closed window and rolls right past them into an underground parking garage.

"Where the hell are we?" I ask.

"Home sweet home."

I scowl. He might have spoken, but his answer tells me nothing.

We cruise to the far end of the garage, and Grey parks the car in a spot marked Reserved. On either side of us, several other Reserved spaces are filled with cars whose retail prices are higher than I know I'll see in my lifetime.

He cuts the engine and climbs out. The moment he does, I glance around for some sign of another person who can help me, but we're utterly alone. A second later, he's pulling my door open and crouching in the opening to look at me.

"I'm going to untape you," he says warily. "And we're going to go upstairs together. Okay?"

"Go fuck yourself."

His eyes narrow. "I wasn't lying earlier. I'm the friend-liest option for you now. If you try to run—and if, by some miracle, you get away from me—whoever finds you will do worse things to you than I have planned."

I shudder, despite the bullshit he's trying to feed me.

"And what exactly do you have planned?" I ask.

He flashes me a smile that's probably meant to scare the shit out of me. "Guess you're about to find out."

The duct tape hurts like hell as he rips it off my skin.

"Son of a bitch," I hiss and attempt to swing on him.

Unfortunately, my arms are still useless. Not quite as limp as before but definitely not packing any punches.

My captor gives me a wry look.

"You'll live," he says simply and then pulls me from the car.

His arm slides around my waist, and he supports me against him as we make our way to an elevator nearby. Walking on my bare feet hurts like hell, thanks to the gravel I sprinted over during my escape attempt earlier. But I'm too stubborn to tell him I can't do it.

Besides, up close, his scent hits me, and I feel the stirring of attraction. It's stupid because, after chasing me through the woods, he should smell like sweat or at least stale cologne. Instead, he smells like sex on legs, and my core heats with an ache of desire.

Refusing to give in to it, I shove my body sideways and bring my foot down on his as hard as I can.

"Dammit," he growls, but his grip on my waist only tightens, which is for the best because throwing myself off balance would have sent me sprawling anyway.

We reach the elevator, and he hits the call button. My heart races as I realize I have seconds left before I'm dragged somewhere no one will ever find me. Sucking in a breath to scream for help one last time, my attempt is thwarted when the elevator door slides open.

I'm dragged inside just as I let loose the scream. Grey covers my mouth with his hand and pushes me backward. My back hits the wall with a thud. His chest presses against mine as he looms in front of me, glaring. Our gazes locked, I watch as his frustration gives way to something else. Something that looks like our lap dance all over again.

The doors slide shut, sealing us in silence.

He removes his hand from my mouth, but he doesn't back off. His other hand is propped above my head as he leans in. We're close enough that I can practically feel his heartbeat. I wonder if he can feel mine thudding wildly against my ribs.

His gaze flicks to my mouth, and every nerve in my body stands on end.

Fear, desire, and need are a war inside me.

My hands and arms tingle as the feeling in them finally returns. Slowly, I lift my palms to his chest and shove. Hard.

He steps back, though I have a feeling it's more by choice than my show of force.

We ride the rest of the way in silence.

By the time the doors open, my bladder has come back online along with the rest of me, and I have to pee so bad it hurts.

Grey moves aside to let me pass, and I do so without hesitation this time. But one glance at our surroundings has me stopping and gawking. The doors have opened to a large penthouse that sprawls straight back, one space flowing into the other. A gray sectional sits before a glass coffee table and faces a large-screen television mounted on the wall. Behind that, sunken a couple of steps below us is a dining table that seats six.

On the left, a bar opens toward a modern kitchen with more gleaming white than I've ever seen in one place. On the right, glass windows make up the entire wall, offering a view of the city with a hazy purple mountain range in the distance.

The view is breathtaking as is the level of luxury inside this apartment.

I turn to look at Grey. "You live here?"

He ignores my question, sidestepping me as he leads the way past the kitchen and down a narrow hallway. "Come on. Your room is this way."

I follow, mostly because my bladder requires it.

The carpet beneath my feet is soft and plush—and gray like the couch and curtains. The dude has a thing for monochrome, clearly. He's just lucky my feet aren't bleeding from all those rocks earlier. They hurt bad enough that I wonder about it, but a quick check at the carpet behind me reveals spotless tracks.

Up ahead, the hallway has two doors on the left and two on the right. Grey opens the last one on the right, and I follow him inside.

"Bathroom's through there," he says, and I dash past him into the shiny bathroom that's nearly as big as the tiny-ass efficiency I've been living in.

The door shuts behind me, and I lock it then hurry up and relieve my aching bladder. When I'm done, I take a second to inspect my reflection. Dark circles ring my eyes, and my hair is a tangled mess. Basically, I look like I've been through a shitstorm. The problem is I'm still in it. And the fear reflected in my tired eyes is proof that this nightmare has only gotten worse from the moment I woke up inside it.

I need a way out.

No one's coming to save me—so I'm going to have to save myself.

Story of my life.

The fear squeezes my heart, but I shove it back. I've been saving myself for as long as I can remember, and I'm somehow still here.

You got this, I whisper to myself.

Then, I open the door and hold my chin high, determined to keep a promise I made to myself years ago: to survive, no matter what.

8

GREY

*H*er question about what I plan to do with her echoes in my mind. I'm probably going to hell for fucking with her when she's clearly already scared of me, but I can't help it. Something about her innocence grates on me. The fact that she doesn't even know what Indigo Hills *is* makes me jealous of her in ways I can't even begin to describe. Not that she'd believe me if I told her. Hell, if she's smart, she'll never believe a word that comes out of my mouth again.

We're enemies.

Even if the scent of her body puts me right back on that couch with her thighs draped over mine and her mouth pouting at me for a kiss. None of that matters when she's my ticket out.

And I don't want anything more than I want to be free.

To remind myself of that very fact, I close myself in my bathroom and send a text to my father.

Made it back. She's all yours.

My stomach twists as I send the last three words.

It's true. She's his pawn to use now.

He won't hurt her, not physically—not when she's so valuable to him alive. But putting her fate in his hands makes me sick.

Almost immediately, he texts back. **Be there soon. Sending extra guards now.**

I wonder if the guards are for her or for me.

Freedom, I remind myself. That's what this is about.

And I'm almost there.

Even as I think it, my chest twinges with guilt. This city has been at the mercy of tyrants and monsters for decades. Growing up, I used to think I could change things. That I could really make a difference. Somewhere along the way, the futility of my desire hit me. Between my father and Franco and their never-ending feud, the people of Indigo Hills are nothing more than collateral damage. Every time I tried to help, I failed. At some point, I stopped fighting for them and decided, if I couldn't save them, I could at least save myself.

My father might have been the one to track me down and order me home, but I only came so that I could find a way to be free of him once and for all. I'm still surprised he agreed to our deal—one last favor for being allowed to leave and never return—but I want it too badly to question his reasons. Guilt tugs at me for what it will mean to see him take over the pack, but I decided long ago that Indigo Hills is a lost cause. Hell, after what I've just done to Lexi, maybe I am too.

9

LEXI

*G*rey's waiting for me when I exit the bathroom. Arms crossed, feet planted, he stands framed by a window with the sunlight muted by a Roman shade. Refusing to acknowledge the fact that I find him handsome as he broods at me, I look away. Instead, I glance over and note the neutral bedroom tones. The space is furnished with a dresser, nightstand, and large bed, the last of which is covered by a fuzzy comforter and matching pillows done in a soft gray. Shocking.

I turn back to my captor and do my best to appear unfazed by my circumstances—something that's getting harder and harder to do as reality sets in.

"Better?" he asks.

"I'm not going to pee on your carpet if that's what you're asking."

He drops his arms, shaking his head as he makes his way to the door. "You're more of a smartass than I expected."

"At least one of us expected this." I glare at him pointedly. "Are you going to tell me what you're planning to do with me? Or do you get off on leaving me terrified at all the possibilities I'm imagining?"

"I don't get off on any of this."

He seemed to get off on that lap dance, I remind myself. Even thinking it makes my cheeks flame with heat, but I refuse to bring that up now.

"Then why kidnap me in the first place?" I demand.

"Because, princess, you're valuable. Whether you know it or not. And I need the leverage you provide me."

I can't help but laugh at his words. "You must have me confused with someone else. I'm not leverage, and I'm no princess. I'm worthless," I say, my voice twisting at how much I hate that it's true. "I'm nothing to anyone. No value at all. Sorry to disappoint, but you've done all this for nothing."

"You're Lexi Ryall. Or that's the name you go by."

"What the hell do you mean *the name I go by*? That's my name, dumbass."

I clamp down on my tongue. Apparently, fear makes me a shit-talker.

His eyes flash, but his voice remains even as he says, "No, your real name is Lexi Giovanni. You're the granddaughter of Franco Giovanni, the alpha of the entire mafia pack and the man who currently runs this city. You are his only living blood relation, and that makes you valuable currency in my world."

His voice is calm and matter-of-fact, but that doesn't stop my jaw from dropping.

"I'm sorry, did you just say mafia?"

"I did."

So, the rumors are true? The mafia is real? And this asshole thinks I'm related to them?

"That's insane. Truly. I mean, I knew you were crazy for kidnapping me, but this story is just... I think you need to check your sources. I don't even have a family. I grew up in foster care. My parents were killed when I—"

"Was three months old," he finishes for me.

I scowl. "Anyone could have looked up that detail."

"You're right. It's in your social services file. What's not in that file is the cause of death."

"Actually, it is. They died in a car accident, wise-ass," I shoot back.

"It does say that. And it's true that they died in the car. But what the file left out was the cause of death being a gunshot wound to the chest. For both of them."

I stare at him in stunned silence.

Four years ago, just before I aged out of the system, my social worker caved and showed me my file. The first and only thing I looked at was the little bit of information they had on my parents, including cause of death. It's the only reason I know the story Grey just gave me is real.

"How do you know that?" I manage to ask.

My stomach twists with the idea that he might be telling the truth. But that's crazy.

"My sources," he said, way too damn smugly, "don't lie."

"Well, I want to talk to these sources," I demand. "Now."

"Not happening. As far as you're concerned, I'm your source for everything."

"You're holding me hostage," I realize. "Or ransom or whatever. Using me against this Franco guy." Grey doesn't answer. "Wait," I say when he starts to leave. "Does he... does Franco know I exist?"

His hard gaze softens ever so slightly. "Yeah," he says quietly. "He's known all along."

"I see."

Hot tears burn my eyes, but I blink them back, refusing to let myself fully believe his story. If I do, it means believing in a grandfather who's known about me all along —and didn't give a shit about what I went through to survive.

The pain hardens into resolve. Fuck him and his resources, which are apparently extensive, given the fact that he runs this town.

Pack, Lexi. He runs a pack of wolves in a secret city in the mountains.

Ugh.

"In that case, what can I do to help?" I ask.

Grey's expression flickers with genuine surprise, and I can see he never considered I'd do this willingly. Now that I've offered, the wheels are clearly turning.

In the end, though, he shakes his head. "You think you want to help, but you don't know what you're agreeing to."

"I know this Franco asshole let me go through a lot of bullshit when he could have saved me from it," I say. "Whatever he did to you, it's not worse than what he did to me."

"Look, it's not really about him," he says warily. "You're the heir to the ruling family in this city. And my family is the only one with enough power and clout to stand a chance against yours."

"Your family wants to take control."

"My family wants to take everything from Franco," he says, that same fury flashing in his eyes.

"And you're going to somehow use me to do that?"

"We already did do that," he corrects. "We took you."

"That's the dumbest plan I've ever heard. I'm nothing to that guy, clearly, considering I've never met him."

"Never meeting him is precisely what tells me you are not nothing."

"What does that even mean?"

He shakes his head. "You'll see. Whether you want to or not, you'll see."

10

GREY

Franco's a son of a bitch. I've always known it, but after meeting Lexi, I'm not sure I can continue giving him credit for the good shit he's done for this town. Not if it meant giving her the life she's had. The look in her eyes when I told her who she was, that she wasn't actually alone on this planet like she thought, and then watching her realize her people didn't want her... I might as well have kicked a puppy.

Her offer to join forces surprised me, but the thing I can't stop thinking about is how much I wanted to take her up on it. I acted like the idea was stupid but honestly? It's what I would have done if I'd been in her shoes. Ally with the bastards holding you prisoner. It's literally a survival technique I learned in my training during my time away. And she did it out of instinct. Or maybe heartfelt desire, I don't know.

Either way, it doesn't matter.

My father won't allow it.

I have to remember this isn't my war. I'm only the one firing the first shot.

When my part is done, I'll vanish again, this time for a lot longer than a few years. This is not an empire I want for myself, not with Franco at the helm and damn sure not with my father running it either. Worry for Indigo Hills tugs at me, for its people who didn't ask for this fight but will be caught in the crossfire nonetheless. I've spent years training to keep innocents out of danger, which is the irony of it all since I just put one right smack the hell in it. But I've made my peace with being the asshole. What's proving a hell of a lot harder is wanting to finish what I started with Lexi on that couch.

The minute I think of it, my body responds, muscles tightening, dick hardening. My wolf stirs, and the feeling of raw need ripping through me nearly brings me to my knees. This is more than attraction or lust. This is primal. I've never felt it before, and I have no idea how to stop it other than to give in—but that's not an option.

Instead, I stalk into my bathroom to turn on the shower —ice cold—and strip, stepping into the steady stream with a hiss between my teeth.

My muscles tense and coil at the onslaught of cold water streaming over my body. Then everything goes limp —which is exactly the fucking point.

I wash quickly and towel off before padding out and into the walk-in closet that attaches to both the bathroom and bedroom. The penthouse is kind of ridiculous and not somewhere I ever spent a lot of time before. Maybe a few times when I wanted to impress girls, but it was never home for me. It's cold and empty—which is a constant reminder of my father's nature and the exact reason I never came here much before now. But between the secure elevator entrance and the guards and cameras we have stationed around the perimeter, the place is a damn fortress. At least, locked in this pristine tower, Lexi's safe from anyone else who'd try to make a move for her.

My phone vibrates and I frown at the unknown number but answer it anyway.

"Yeah."

"Grey," says a soft female voice that I recognize instantly.

"Mom. What—Where are you?"

"Your father said you made it back."

My brows lift. "You're talking to him again? You said last time was it—"

She sighs. "My whole life is here, darling."

Something about the way she says it. "You're back, aren't you?"

"Yes." There's defeat in that single word but also determination. "You know how it is."

I resist the urge to punch something. "Yeah. Guess I do."

"You're safe? You're not hurt?"

Her worry tugs an almost-smile from me as I picture Lexi actually inflicting any damage on me. "I'm not hurt," I assure her.

"Good. Listen, I know you're in the middle of something for your father right now, but when you're done, you need to come for dinner. I haven't gotten enough time with you since you've been back."

"That's because I was here all of twenty-four hours before the old man sent me out on this mission."

"And before that, you were gone for five years. You owe your mother a meal."

Her tone takes on a stern lecture quality that has me giving in to the guilt tugging at me for leaving her in the first place. She's not the one I wanted to get away from, but she undoubtedly suffered for it.

"Tell you what, when I'm done with all this, I'll come pick you up, and we'll drive out to that bed and breakfast you like. We'll stay a few days, maybe go to a winery."

"Hmm." She hesitates. "Don't think I don't know what you're doing. Trying to get me away from here."

Not here. Him.

"I don't care if you know," I say honestly.

She sighs. "All right, sweetie. We'll go there. You and me."

"You and me," I echo.

A noise from Lexi's bedroom interrupts.

"Mom, I have to go," I tell her.

"Okay, love you, sweetie."

"Love you, too."

I hang up, and my gaze lands on the selection of suits hanging in a row in my closet, all of them undoubtedly delivered here at my father's request, but I step past them and snag another pair of pants and shirt like the ones I wore earlier instead. They're more casual and comfortable, but they're also better for tucking weapons inside them than a damned suit is. Something my father never understood or cared about and something I'm done trying to explain. He got me back here for one last job, but he's not going to get anything else.

After this, I'm done.

11

LEXI

Grey doesn't lock the door behind him, but the sentiment is clear. Alone, I prowl the bedroom for several minutes, my thoughts crashing into one another as I process everything he just told me.

A wolf pack mafia.

It's a lot to take in, but despite the impossibility of men becoming actual wolves, it's that last word I keep coming back to.

Two days ago, I would have laughed at the very suggestion that I might somehow be involved in the mafia. Maybe because, whenever I think of the mafia, I picture guys with Jersey accents and gold chains busting kneecaps with baseball bats. I'm not that.

But then, neither is Grey.

And while he's shown me no proof that his story about me is real, something tells me he's not lying about the dark world he's grown up inside. It's in his eyes. Every time I look into them, I see glimpses of shadows and secrets best left buried.

Grey's the kind of guy who backs up his talk with action.

Even as I think the words, a thrill shoots down my spine.

Not that kind of action, I tell myself.

Ugh.

I force myself to refocus on the problem of, you know, being kidnapped. Even if my kidnapper is dripping sex appeal, I still have to figure out a way to get free before I become a pawn in his criminal game.

There's only one problem.

If I really am an heir to a crime syndicate, then being trapped inside this room is nothing compared to what waits for me out there. I suddenly remember Grey warned me that being held captive by him was probably the safest option in this city. And that makes me trapped on a whole new level. Even if I find a way out of this apartment, I won't be any safer; not while I'm inside the borders of Indigo Hills.

Still, I can't exactly sit around, twiddling my thumbs, waiting for someone to show up and rescue me. That's never happening—not to me.

If I'm going to get out of this shit, I'll have to save myself.

Despite Grey's warning, I glance around for some way out. Survival instincts and all that. But the one window in the room is locked tight, and even if it weren't, I'm twenty floors up at least with no fire escape or even a ledge or drain pipe to help.

Ugh.

If I want to be free, I have to start by leaving this room.

When my stomach growls, I decide it's as good an excuse as any to venture out, if for no other reason than to test the boundaries of my cage.

Grey's in the kitchen, dressed in a fresh shirt and dark cargo pants that are nearly identical to what he wore earlier. His dark hair is wet, and I can smell his soap as I drift closer, stopping in front of the bar that separates me from the kitchen—and him.

The smell of him alone threatens to make me forget he's my enemy.

"Figured you'd be asleep," he says, eyeing me.

"Figured you'd have locked me in that room," I shoot back.

"No need. Elevator's fingerprint operated."

Damn.

"So, I'll have to kill you or cut off your hand to get out of here."

His brow lifts at that, but the lack of worry as he dismisses the comment and turns for the fridge makes it clear he doesn't see me as a threat.

Asshole.

"You hungry?" he asks, taking out a carton of eggs.

My stomach growls again, and I suddenly hate how I'm completely at his mercy. "I could eat."

His mouth quirks, and then he goes to work scrambling eggs like he's done it a thousand times. I slide onto a barstool to watch, catching myself admiring the flexing of his forearm muscles as he whips the eggs, adding a little milk and some herbs.

"So," I say, trying for casual. "You're in the mafia."

He nods but doesn't look up.

"What's it like?"

"The benefits suck," he quips.

"Have you killed anyone before?" I ask as he pours the eggs into a hot pan.

He glances at me then back down again. "Have you?"

That's not an answer, but it's also not the most important question.

"Are you going to kill *me*?"

He looks up then, spatula in one hand, and meets my eyes with a level gaze. "No," he says firmly, and even though I know it's probably naive of me, I believe him. "That's not on the table," he adds.

The way he says it makes me wonder if someone wanted it on the table.

"Was kidnapping me your idea?" I ask.

He doesn't answer, which, even without words, tells me this isn't his plan. It also explains why he's not locking me in a room or tying me to a chair.

"Here," he says, handing me a plate of eggs and a fork. "Eat."

I take the fork, but I also continue watching him as he pours coffee and juice, offering them both to me. The longer I'm around this guy, the more I wonder how he came to be someone who'd kidnap another human. Because beneath his grouchy exterior, he doesn't seem like a bad guy.

Or maybe I just have Stockholm's Syndrome already.

"What?" he asks, and I realize I've been openly staring for way too long.

"I'm just wondering why you really brought me here."

"Believe me, I'm wondering the same thing. I had no idea you wouldn't have an off switch."

I smile at that. "I've been told I could talk a hole in your head."

"A deadly weapon," he mutters, and for some reason, knowing I'm annoying him makes me feel better. If I can't fight my way out, maybe I can talk him to death.

"Seriously," I push. "You don't seem like the kidnapping type."

"You don't know me."

"And you don't know me, but you keep calling me princess as if I've somehow lived a life of luxury despite being orphaned, broke, and alone my entire life."

He scowls. "You don't know how lucky—"

The elevator dings, and he breaks off, his head swiveling toward the entrance. When he looks back at me, there's mild panic reflected in his gaze.

"I thought you said it only takes your fingerprint," I say, confused.

"Mine or my father's." His voice is grim enough to send a ripple of unease down my spine. "Go to your room. Don't come out until I tell you."

I slide off my stool and do as he says, some instinct telling me not to argue with him on this one. Just as I slip into my room, the elevator dings again, and I hear the hum of the doors sliding open. Leaving my door cracked, I hover in the opening, listening.

In the main living area, another male voice says, "Where is she?"

"In the spare room," Grey says. His voice is different now, more guarded than he was with me.

"What? You're not going to offer me a drink?"

"What would you like?"

Grey's voice is strained, and it piques my curiosity. After how dominating he's been with me, I can't help but wonder why he's suddenly being so different.

Out in the living area, I hear the man say, "Club soda."

The fridge opens, and I use the sound of a glass clinking to ease open my bedroom door and pad into the hall.

The ice machine goes off, cubes clinking into the glass, and I inch forward, easing down the hall so I can peek around toward the visitors. The water dispenser runs, and then footsteps sound. I wait until Grey's out of the kitchen and then take another step.

There's a pause, and then the visitor snaps, "You let her eat out here?"

The harshness of his tone makes me jump.

"What does it matter?" Grey says in that same strained tone as before. "She can't leave."

The visitor snorts at that, ice clinking again as the glass moves. "Just as well. There's a change in plans. It might be good to spend a bit of time with her."

I ease forward another inch, and the stranger's shoulder comes into view. He's sitting on the couch, his back to me. Same color hair as Grey with a few gray streaks. It's shorter than Grey's, slicked back and shiny. The suit he wears hugs his broad shoulders and wide torso like it's custom-made for him. He's leaning forward slightly, the water glass on the coffee table between him and his son.

"What change?" Grey sounds wary now.

I wait silently as the stranger, his father, responds.

"Franco knows we have her."

"Dammit, how the hell—" Grey breaks off and swears then says, "I told you we had a rat."

"Regardless of who leaked it, Franco's got his own people spreading the news that we've taken his grand-daughter."

I get a look at the back of the man's head. Dark hair, broad shoulders, black suit. Strong cologne wafts toward me, and I wrinkle my nose.

"Are you serious? The man's truly lost it then. He's only making himself look weak—"

"No, he's making us look like assholes," the man snaps.

Grey's gaze flicks to me. The moment he sees me, his eyes widen, and he looks quickly back at his father.

"We can't afford public opinion to shift," the man goes on. "Not after all the work we've done to position ourselves this way."

"There's not much we can do considering it's true." Grey's expression is hard now. He's purposely not looking at me, but a muscle in his jaw is twitching.

He's pissed.

"Not we, you," his father says pointedly. "And yes, there is something."

"Forget it. I'm out," Grey says viciously enough that I take a step back. He goes on, his words laced with fury. "I came back here and did this one last favor for you, but that's it. I'm not part of this—"

"Bullshit!" The man shoves to his feet, towering over his son. "You're part of this family, like it or not, boy." His tone is cruel now. Angry. "You can pretend otherwise, but that won't stop the shitstorm from landing on your doorstep just as much as mine. Or have you forgotten you are the one who brought her here in the first place?" He pauses as if to let it sink in. "It's you they want now, not me."

"You fucked me," Grey says quietly. "On purpose."

His father doesn't acknowledge the accusation. "One way or another, you're involved. At least, playing offense means you're in control."

"I should have known there'd never just be one favor with you." Grey's tone is bitter. "What do you want from me now?"

"You're going to convince that bitch to marry you."

I make a noise of surprise, and the man whirls, giving me a clear view of his face. And him of me.

Shit.

Up close, I see that he and Grey do share a physical resemblance, but where the elder might have been handsome once, there's a callous expression etched across his face that is deeply lined as if he wears it permanently.

"What the fuck are you doing out here?" he demands.

The cruelty in his eyes sharpens to daggers at the sight of me, and I shrink back against the far wall, silent.

Grey jumps up, heading off his father as the large man rounds the sofa toward me.

"I told you, she can't leave, so what's the point of locking her in a room?" Grey says, sliding between me and his father.

"The point is that this conversation is none of her damn business." The man stops, looming over both of us.

"It's my business if it's about me," I say, the words tumbling out before I can hold them back.

At my words, the man's eyes gleam in a way that makes

me want to shrink all over again. "All right, sweetheart. We'll play it your way."

"Don't," Grey begins.

"No, she's got a right." He waves Grey aside and puts out his hand. "I'm Vincenzo Diavolo."

I step around Grey and shake the man's hand, pretending I'm not trembling with fear. "Lexi Ryall."

His grip is already firm, but the moment he has full hold of my hand, he squeezes—tightly. I grit my teeth, wincing as the pain threatens to drag a scream from my throat.

"Enough," Grey snaps, and Vincenzo lets go.

I exhale and snatch my hand away again, stepping back so that I'm standing shoulder-to-shoulder with the asshole's son. It's stupid considering I'm technically a prisoner of both of them.

"Glad to see you're not some wilting little flower," Vincenzo says, scanning me like he's sizing me up.

"Glad to see you're the asshole I thought you'd be," I fire back.

It's stupid of me to cross him when he clearly has zero fucks to give about me, but I can't stop myself. No wonder Grey told me to wait in the bedroom. He's a bigger asshole than I could have imagined—even with all the horrible mafia stereotypes in mind.

Grey tenses beside me, but Vincenzo just throws his head back and laughs uproariously.

"She's a firecracker, isn't she?" he says.

"No argument there," Grey mutters.

I ignore it and cross my arms, refusing to let this man see me sweat.

"I'm not going to just let you do this to me," I say.

He stares at me, still smiling. "And who's going to fucking stop me?"

"Sir," Grey says wearily. "She's right. Marriage? That's insane."

I snort, because *same.*

"It's the only way to convince Franco's pack we didn't kidnap her," Vincenzo says. "That she came willingly."

"But I didn't," I say, glaring. "And the moment you put me in front of someone willing to listen, that's exactly what I'll tell them."

His eyes flash, and then he moves so fast I don't see it coming until he's backed me against the wall and leaned in, his face so close to mine that I can smell the club soda on his breath.

"You listen to me, you little bitch," he snarls. "This might have started with your piece of shit grandpa, but I'll finish it with you, and I won't lose a single fucking night's sleep doing it. Your family is done running this town, and you can either get on board, or we'll get rid of you entirely. The choice is yours, but I suggest you make it fast, or that pretty little mouth of yours won't be alive long enough to run itself to anyone again."

"Stop!"

Grey shoves Vincenzo, and I watch as the surprise of it sends the asshole side-stepping away from me. He recovers fast, glaring at his son. Something passes between them, a crackle of energy that paralyzes me despite wanting to flee back to my room. Anywhere to be away from the monsters before me. Instead, I watch, unable to look away, as Grey stares his father down, hands fisted and trembling.

Vincenzo takes a single step toward us again and then stops.

"Don't you ever put your hands on me like that again," he warns.

"Lexi, go to your room," Grey says.

I decide to do as he asks without argument, slipping away before Vincenzo can object.

At the end of the hall, I step into my room and go still, listening.

Both men are silent for another long moment, making my imagination run wild with what I can't see. Maybe they've both shifted into wolves. Maybe they're going to tear each other apart limb from limb right there on the luxury carpet.

Maybe—

"You can't ask me to do this," Grey says, and desperation leaks into his tone, driving out the fury from before. "Not with her."

I tense, unable to avoid the little ping of hurt his words cause.

Stupid.

He doesn't even know me.

And I hate him.

Why should I care if he doesn't want to marry me?

I damn sure don't want to marry him either.

"You gave your word you'd help this family get to the top," Vincenzo says darkly. "This is how you do that. So, stop fucking whining about it."

"You asked me to bring her here. To use her as leverage to make the old man hand over the reins. That was our deal. You never said anything about marriage."

"Well, I'm saying it now."

"That wasn't the agreement."

"And plans change, boy. Get over it."

"You're a son of a bitch," Grey says.

The answering *crack* is so loud I wonder if the bar broke in half. Unable to help myself, I peer out and down the hall—then go still as I watch Grey straightening from where his whole body was driven sideways. When he straightens, a large, reddish bruise is already forming just below his eye.

Holy shit. Vincenzo hit him?

I brace myself for what Grey will do in return, but he only glares back at his father, eyes blazing with the fires of Hell.

"She won't do it," Grey says.

"Then change her damn mind," Vincenzo booms. "Make her fall for your sorry ass. Do whatever you have to."

"You want me to manipulate her into actually liking me?"

Vincenzo looms over his son, poking Grey in the chest. "I don't give a shit what you say or do; just get it done. You have three days before we go public with this, and she needs to be on board, or she's useless to me."

Vincenzo shoves past him and heads for the door.

Grey barks out a laugh. "This is insane. I can't do it. I won't."

Vincenzo spins and growls, the sound of it vibrating through the walls, shaking the artwork, and coming up through the carpet at my feet. "You'll do it, or you'll suffer the same consequences Franco's son did."

I shudder at the open violence in the man's tone. But

Vincenzo doesn't wait for an answer before he stalks toward the elevator with the confidence of a man expecting to be obeyed.

When Grey finally speaks again, his voice is hard and controlled. "This is the last favor I do for you, old man. When we're done, I don't ever want to see your face again."

"It'll be no loss to me," Vincenzo scoffs. "And my advice? Use protection when you do your convincing. Who knows what she picked up from that club before you yanked her worthless ass out."

A second later, the elevator door dings, and the hum of the doors sound.

Then, the apartment is quiet.

Minutes tick by.

I don't move, waiting to see if Grey will come to get me. But he doesn't appear, and there's no sound from the living room.

I emerge slowly, making my way down the hall with my heart in my throat.

Marriage... to Grey? No way. It's not like my life was anything special before, but that doesn't mean I'm going to tie myself forever to a man willing to toss me into a trunk.

He's on the couch, his head hung low, his hands propped on his knees.

When I step into the room, he lifts his eyes to mine, and the look he wears punches me in the gut. I see nothing but pure, raw pain, and layered over that is utter hatred.

"If that's what family's like, I guess I'm better off." It's a horrible joke, but the bleakness in his eyes lightens just a little anyway.

"Yours is no picnic either," he shoots back.

"So you say."

He drops his head again. A moment of silence passes between us.

"Would he really kill you?" I ask quietly, but I think I already know the answer when he snorts.

"Who knows at this point."

I bite my lip, thrown by the idea that a father could kill his own son. I've never had a family before, but I've always imagined something, well, better than this.

"Will he be home anytime soon?" I ask, already dreading a round two with that asshole.

He looks up, his brows furrowing. "He doesn't live here."

"Oh. I thought—"

"My father has multiple houses so that he can be in one while his family members are at another." His voice twists in a way that tells me he's learned this the hard way.

"Do you have siblings?" I ask, finding myself wanting to know more about this guy—as fucked up as he is.

He shakes his head then looks down again. "No, and that's a good thing. I don't want to think about what it would be like to watch anyone else be hurt."

I want to ask what he means by that because there's a haunted look in his eyes that is at odds with his answer. Instead, it makes me think about my family. The parents I never knew and apparently were taken from me, thanks to my supposed grandfather.

"Did Franco really kill my dad?" I ask.

He looks up at me again. "That's the rumor."

I sink onto the oversized chair beside me. The leather is

cold enough to make me shiver—or maybe it's the hard truths that have been continuously dumped on me today.

Grey's sharp eyes don't miss it. "Cold?"

"A little."

He hesitates then reaches over and pulls a blanket off the back of the couch. Then he stands, makes his way over to me, and drapes the blanket across my lap.

"Thanks," I tell him softly. He sits again, and I shake my head. "You don't seem like a mafia type."

His brow arches. "I wasn't aware there's a type. Or that you know so many of us already."

"I just mean… my friend Violet, her brother took a loan from a mafia guy in Indigo Hills once. Apparently, he couldn't repay it on time and was never seen again. I thought you were all criminals and murderers."

"What makes you think I'm not those things?"

"Your dad is scary and mean. He sounds like a killer. But you…"

I trail off, biting my lip as my thoughts jumble on the possible ways to end that sentence.

He leans forward so that our knees are nearly touching. "What about me?"

"You're not scary."

It's not exactly true, but I can't bring myself to explain that Grey scares me in ways that have nothing to do with physical harm.

His mouth tightens. "Guess I'm not trying hard enough."

"Apparently, you're not supposed to be trying at all," I point out. "According to the new plan, you're supposed to be convincing me to marry you."

I expect him to rant or get pissed all over again. Something involving backing away from me because I really need some space right now. But he only leans closer, cocking his head to one side in a smug sort of challenge as his closeness sucks all the air from between us.

"Is that what you want, princess? For me to convince you to want me?"

My heart stutters at the way he looks at me now. Hungry. Like a predator who wants to eat me—and in this particular case, I might just want to be eaten.

I think of the lap dance, and it pisses me off.

"You already tried that, and it didn't work," I toss back.

His smirk tells me he knows exactly what I'm talking about—and recognizes the lie for what it is. "I'd say it worked pretty well considering you're sitting here now."

I glare. "Only because you kidnapped me afterward."

"You made it so easy, darlin'," he drawls. "Running slow and then pretending to faint so I'd have to carry you against my naked body." He winks, and my temper spikes. "Was it as good for you as it was for me?"

Heat shoots through me at his words, but I refuse to acknowledge my body's reaction. "You abducted me from my home," I snap. "Tied me up and threw me in your trunk. No, it was not good for me."

"Home, huh? And what exactly is waiting for you back there?"

"Friends," I snap. "And people who need me."

"Right. You keep telling yourself that while you sit in this luxury penthouse in a city your family practically owns. Your life is so terrible, isn't it?"

"You know what? I take it all back. You're a complete asshole."

His smirk widens, but it's more a flash of teeth than a smile, like he's reminding me what a predator he really is. "You keep acting like I'm supposed to be some saint, but the proof is right in front of you, darling." His voice twists with sarcasm on the last word. "Your future husband is as dark-hearted as they come. Better get used to it."

12

GREY

From the balcony of my bedroom, I stare out over the twinkling city lights. One hand grips the railing with more force than necessary. With the other, I take a sip of the whiskey I've been nursing for an hour. From up here, the twinkling city of Indigo Hills looks harmless, but I know better. I'm not nearly as naïve as my father thinks I am, which is why I saw this coming from the moment he first tracked me down a month ago.

I knew then he wouldn't let me walk away as easily as he promised. There's never just one favor with him. I assumed all along he'd do something fucked up to keep me reeled into his schemes. To punish me for mine. Still, I never thought he'd pull some shit like this.

Marriage.

To a Giovanni?

He can go fuck himself.

Unfortunately, I know him well enough to know, if I refuse, he'll just find someone else who'll go along with his crazy, fucked up plan. His threat about killing me is empty.

He knows it and I know it. He'll torture me, make me wish I was dead, but he won't kill me.

The real threat is what he'll do to Lexi. I don't need my wolf's sixth sense to know he's already realized I care what happens to her.

The moment I stepped between them earlier, I gave away my weakness, and the game has barely even started.

I take another drink, staring blindly at the twinkling lights of the city I once called home. Indigo Hills isn't a bad place for most of its residents. Whatever monster he might be personally, Franco at least sees to that. The economy is thriving, employment is up, and the community is tight-knit. Or it has been until recently.

Something is happening behind the scenes, and no one knows what. All we know for sure is that things have started to slip. First, a business owner got roughed up for not paying enough "taxes" to his "local representative." Then, four elementary schools lost their funding for their music and arts programs. An audit of the city planner's office showed that the budget was reallocated to the Giovanni Foundation, which is Franco's smokescreen for discretionary spending on himself and his hired men.

It's bullshit. And it's exactly the kind of thing I've always wanted to stop in this town. I only ever walked away because Franco finally seemed to settle into something resembling decent. For the last few years, he at least did a better job than my old man would have, and that's enough for me.

Now, that's no longer true, and something has to be done.

Unfortunately, some*thing* has become a some*one*.

After twenty years as Giovanni's biggest rival, my father is perfectly poised to do what no one else has ever attempted. He's going to unseat the alpha of the mafia pack and put himself on that throne instead. Using Lexi to do it is just a practical means to an end. Or it was until I met her.

Now that I have, I'm not sure I can let one monster replace another. Not if it means hurting her in the process. For reasons I can't understand, my wolf won't allow it, and I'm not sure there's any difference between him and me on this one.

My phone vibrates, and I see Dutch's name on the screen.

"What?" I answer.

"We found Trucker."

"It's late, bro. You couldn't call me in the morning to tell me that?"

"We found him with a girl. Maybe sixteen?"

"Dammit." Anger heats my blood, and the need to punch that asshole myself makes my knuckles ache. "Is she okay?"

"She will be. Could use a softer touch than Razor and Crow, though."

I sigh because I know who he wants me to call. "Where's Mia now?"

"Not answering her phone," he says, clearly annoyed.

I sigh again. "Did he at least give you any details on what he's fed Franco?"

His voice drops low. "He says he'll only talk to the princess herself."

"You've got to be fucking kidding me," I say. "Now?"

"That's what he says. We're at the cargo dump. You want me to stay put?"

"Yeah, keep him there. I'm on my way."

I hang up and toss back the rest of my drink. This town is going to be the death of me yet.

13

LEXI

I sleep with a chair wedged beneath the knob of my bedroom door. Okay, not so much sleep as lie in the dark, trying to make myself relax. It doesn't come easily, thanks to my racing thoughts. After all that's happened, I don't know whether to be more scared of the mafia head that never wanted me in the first place or the monster of a man trying to force me to marry his son so he can take power.

Two days ago, my biggest worry was earning enough money for rent while somehow not selling my soul in exchange. Now, I'd gladly sell my soul if it means not signing my body over to a man whose worst nightmare is being tied to me forever.

My heart squeezes as I imagine a life with the man sleeping across the hall from me. He's not quite the monster his father is—or at least, I haven't seen that side of him yet. But I can't let myself forget that, at the end of the day, he's my enemy.

If I'm going to survive this, I need to remember that

and stop looking for proof he's the nice guy when all the evidence I have says otherwise.

Hours later, I'm just drifting off when a noise jolts me awake again. It's a soft chime, but in the stillness, it echoes, rattling my nerves. I sit up, listening intently as the chime comes again then abruptly cuts short.

Grey's voice is muffled through the walls. I hear him, but I can't make out the words.

Sliding out of bed, I pad to my door and pull the chair out of the way. Easing the door open, I step into the hall and hover at his door, straining to listen.

"...got to be fucking kidding me," he growls. "Now?"

There's a pause and a snort, and I realize the chime I heard must have been his phone because whoever he's talking to is clearly not in the room with him.

"Yeah, keep him there. I'm on my way."

His response sends me scooting backward, but a second later, his bedroom door flies open. Grey frowns at the sight of me, and I regret putting on the large shirt and oversized shorts he gave me to sleep in. It's the only change of clothes I've been provided, and they smell like him, which only makes it worse. But the only other option was sleeping in the clothes I came here in, which are beyond gross at this point.

"What are you doing up?" he asks.

"Couldn't sleep."

He brushes past me. "Just as well," he says over his shoulder as he starts down the hall toward the kitchen. "Get dressed. We're going out."

I glare at his retreating back. "I am dressed," I say dryly, "Since I currently only own the clothes I arrived in and they're gross."

He stops and turns back, blinking as if he's only just now realized this fact.

I cross my arms.

"Wait here."

He disappears into his bedroom and returns a moment later with a pair of sweatpants.

"Put these on."

"No."

His jaw tightens. "We don't have time for this. Put them on, and let's go."

"I'm not going anywhere until you tell me what's going on."

He hisses out a breath between clenched teeth. "There was supposed to be a supply delivery before you arrived, but it was delayed. I'll have some clothes brought in for you soon. For now, I need you to wear these or put your own clothes back on."

Without waiting for my response, he disappears around the corner toward the living room, and I follow, fully intending on arguing further. He might have kidnapped me, but I refuse to comply with his every wish. I round the corner just in time to see him emerge from a storage closet near the elevator. He's lifted his shirt, revealing abs that make my mouth go suddenly dry so he can tuck a gun into a holster he's strapped across his ribs.

He looks up, and I realize I've just been caught staring.

Swallowing hard, I look away. "What's that for?"

"Hopefully nothing." He stares at me. "Put on the pants, Lexi."

I lift my chin. "No, thanks. I'll wear this."

He stares at me for a long moment then turns for the elevator. "Fine."

He pushes the call button. The door opens, and he looks back at me pointedly.

"Get in."

I cross my arms. "No."

He glares at me, but I don't move. Fuck him and his orders. As much as I want out of this tower, I'm not sure where we're going is any safer.

"Lexi," he warns, but I shake my head.

"I'm not going to let you order me—"

He closes the distance and grabs me, slinging me over his shoulder before I can get away. I shriek, pounding my fists against his back as he carries me onto the elevator.

"Let me go!"

He sets me on my feet, and I immediately lunge for the exit, but he blocks me, caging me in. Behind him, the elevator doors slide shut, and we begin to descend.

"You can come willingly, or I can tie you up and put you in the damned trunk again. The choice is yours."

My heart races, and I'm suddenly very aware of our closeness—and the fact that I'm not wearing a bra beneath this thin shirt. My nipples harden, and I glance from his fiery glare to his full mouth hovering mere inches from mine.

"Lexi."

The sound of him speaking my name sends a shudder through me. When I look up at him again, his eyes flash with something different than the fury I saw a moment ago. It reminds me of the way he watched me when I danced for him. For some reason, it's enough to break the spell.

I clear my throat, looking away from him so I can get my bearings.

"Fine. I'll go."

He hesitates another moment and then, apparently satisfied, steps back. I cross my arms, partly from stubbornness and partly to hide the fact that my body clearly doesn't understand the situation. Every square inch of my skin tingles even though every brain cell in my head screams at it to cut that shit out.

We finish the descent in silence.

Now that he's not crowding me, I remember the gun he strapped to his body before we left. Immediately, my mind begins to conjure all the possible reasons a deadly wolf shifter might also need a gun. Or why we're going out at three in the morning in the first place. Maybe they've decided against using me and are skipping right to the part where they get rid of me entirely. I try to shut out the images, but my brain is on a roll, and I can't shake the idea that certain death awaits me.

Grey takes my arm as the elevator opens to the parking garage. I don't fight him, but my steps are slow as I let him lead me out. Cool air hits me first. Then I catch sight of the two guards posted nearby, and I regret my clothing choice —not that I'll let myself admit that now. Grey ignores the men as he leads me toward his car and opens the front passenger door.

He gestures at me. "Get in."

"I get to ride up front this time?"

"You prefer the trunk?"

I sigh and get in.

He comes around and slides into the driver's seat, the leather crunching as he settles in. The interior is cool, and I rub my arms against the late-night chill.

"Cold?" he asks.

I don't answer.

He starts the car and immediately reaches over, turning up the heat and aiming all the vents at me. Then, he backs us out of the space and cruises toward the gated exit.

Outside the garage, the city is quiet. There are very few cars on the road, and again I'm struck by how peaceful the city feels at this hour. An illusion, I remind myself. All the bad guys are doing their evil deeds at home rather than on the street.

Glancing over at Grey's set jaw and tense shoulders, I realize all but one is home.

When we stop at a red light, I eye the door handle, calculating how far I'd get if I made a run for it.

"This town is full of shifters, and all the humans know."

His words startle me out of my crazy planning. I look over, and the minute our eyes meet, I know he's read my thoughts.

"Why are you telling me that?" I ask.

"Because, as a human, I'm faster than you, but as a wolf, there's nowhere you can hide that I won't track you."

"It's dark as shit out there. How can you track me if you don't see me?" I challenge.

His voice is husky as he says, "I'd know your scent anywhere in the world."

I swallow hard and fix my gaze straight ahead. "Whatever."

The light turns green, and he guns it, propelling us onward.

A series of turns lands us in what looks like an industrial area. Warehouses surrounded by chain link fences capped in barbed wire line the back roads where we wind our way along. Finally, Grey pulls in at one of them. The guard house is empty, so we blow past it and come to a stop before a bay door that's pulled shut.

The minute he parks, the warehouse's side door opens, and a male figure swathed in shadows motions for Grey to hurry up.

He climbs out and hurries around to my side of the car, yanking my door open impatiently.

"Come on."

"I'd rather wait here."

"Not happening."

"I don't have shoes."

He glances at my socked feet. "Your choice," he reminds me.

Asshole.

I climb out, my heart thudding as he takes my arm and pulls me toward the door where the stranger waits. The only thing I can tell from here is that it's not Vincenzo. More scenarios run through my mind, each one worse than the last. Maybe Grey's rejecting his dad's offer to marry me by having me killed off in secret. Maybe he got tired of keeping me at the apartment, so this is my new prison and new guard. Or maybe he's selling me to the highest bidder of his enemies. Either way, nothing good can come of me stepping foot in a warehouse with two men at three a.m.

But before I know it, I'm through the doorway and standing before a tall, lanky male with wavy brown hair whose eyes flash with the promise of violence. My pulse speeds, making me wonder exactly who that violence is meant for.

"Hey, boss," he greets Grey.

"Where's the douchebag?" Grey demands.

"This way." The stranger leads the way, and their footsteps echo over concrete floors as we start down an empty hall. "What's she doing here?" he asks over his shoulder.

"I can't leave her alone."

"Not like she can get out of the tower," the guy points out.

"No, but my father can get in."

"Damn, the old man's being a pain already, huh."

"He can't help himself," Grey says.

The stranger snorts. "Sounds about right. Here we are."

He stops before a door and gestures with a nod. "You ready?"

"Just open the damn door," Grey mutters.

The stranger does as he asks then steps back. Grey lets me go and walks inside. I hesitate, but the sharp-eyed stranger is right behind me, pressing in close enough to send me shuffling forward.

The room is lit by a single work lamp someone's brought in and plugged into an extension cord in the far corner. I'm surprised to see three others already waiting inside.

Two more men stand along the wall to my right. One is tall with cropped, dark hair, deep brown eyes, and defined biceps. The other is shorter with longer hair that hangs in his eyes, though there's a definite resemblance between them.

"Razor. Crow," Grey greets.

"Brother," the taller, more muscled of the two returns.

The second is silent.

Grey ignores the fourth figure but I can't help but stare. A girl, fifteen, maybe sixteen, huddles in the corner on the other side of the two men. Her shirt is torn open, and she holds her arms crossed over her chest to cover herself. She meets my eyes, and the fear that rolls off her is unmistakable. I look from her to the two guys standing between us, and my eyes narrow.

Without waiting for instructions, I shove past the two guys and walk up to the scared girl.

"Hey," I say softly.

Her eyes widen at the sight of me, but she holds her ground as she returns, "Hey," in a small voice.

"Are you hurt?" I ask.

She shakes her head.

I exhale. "Who did this to you?" I ask.

She doesn't answer, but her eyes dart over my shoulder. I turn and follow the direction of her glance. Nearly obscured by shadows, I spot another figure in the far corner of the room.

Blinking through the grainy half-light, I see that an older man sits on the dirty concrete, his head hanging, his long hair obscuring his face. Blood and saliva drip from his mouth. I hadn't even noticed him at first with the way he's hunched over and out of the reach of the lamp's light.

"He did this?" I ask the girl.

"Yes," she whispers.

At her reply, the man raises his head and looks up at us through swollen, bruised lids. His lip curls at the sight of Grey, but then his eyes land on me, and something sparks.

"Well, what do we have here?" The words are muffled by what sounds like a swollen lip. "Royalty has arrived. Now it's a party."

"It's your fucking funeral, Trucker." Grey's voice is colder than I've ever heard. Beside me, the girl flinches. I step closer to her and whisper, "It's going to be all right," despite the fact that I'm just as fucked as she is. I haven't been roughed up, but I'm still a prisoner here.

She doesn't know that, though, and right now, I want only to make her feel safe. My chest pangs at how much she reminds me of one of the shelter teens—and how I might never see any of them again.

"Did she give her statement?" Grey asks, bringing me back to the present nightmare.

"She did," his friend confirms. The lanky one who walked us in here glances over at me as he says it. Our eyes meet, and I see curiosity reflected back at me. But not confusion. He clearly knows who I am. In fact, I get the sense that everyone in this room knows more about me than I do—except the girl.

Cautiously, I slide my hand into hers. She wraps her cold fingers around mine instantly, and I feel a rush of protection toward her.

"That girl doesn't know what she's talking about," Trucker says, eyes narrowing as Grey and his friends discuss what to do about the girl.

"What's your name?" I whisper.

"Claire."

I give her hand a reassuring squeeze. "I'm Lexi. It's going to be okay."

"You're Lexi?" She stares at me with shock and a definite layer of fear that wasn't there a moment ago.

I stiffen.

Across the room, the injured man, Trucker, snorts. "The princess has returned." When I look over at him, he's staring right at me. "Bet you didn't expect such a warm welcome." His wink ruffles me more than I want to admit.

"What are we doing here?" I snap at Grey. "He clearly attacked her. She shouldn't have to be subjected to standing in the same room as him for another second."

Grey turns back to the old man. "You got what you wanted. Now, say what you have to say so judgment can be delivered."

"Not until she comes closer," he says, "I need to look into her eyes and know that it's her."

I hesitate, but Grey, looking pissed enough to murder, waves me forward. I let go of Claire's hand and reluctantly step forward until I'm standing beside Grey.

"That's far enough," he says, his warm shoulder brushing mine.

It's comforting, knowing he's right here with me, which is beyond stupid. The enemy of my enemy does not make him my friend.

"What am I—" I begin, but Grey cuts me off.

"This asshole's been feeding information to Franco," he explains. "He claims he has information for you that he'd only deliver face to face."

"What information?" I ask.

Grey gives the man a pointed look. "Spill it."

"You don't look like an heir to an empire," he says to me.

And even though I couldn't agree more, his words make me feel inadequate and embarrassed.

"Thanks for the vote of confidence. I really care about the predator vote," I tell him.

He laughs—or tries to, it turns quickly into a cough that spews more blood and saliva down his chin.

I resist the urge to step back.

"Ah, you're a Giovanni after all, I see."

I don't answer.

"The old man never wanted it this way, you know."

I stiffen. "So, giving me up for adoption and never coming to find me or tell me I had family was an accident?"

"He was protecting you."

"From what?" I ask.

I have no idea if this guy is speaking the truth, but with so little information to go on, I'll take whatever scrap I can get. Even from a stranger in a warehouse in the middle of the night.

"What the hell do you even know about Franco's intentions?" Grey's friend demands. "You're a sewer rat. A fucking traitor. You can't possibly know what Franco wants."

"As a matter of fact, Franco invited me to have a seat at the table," Trucker says. "He believes those of us who've put in our time should get something in return, which is more than I can say for what this family's given me."

"We've given you a life, a home, protection." Grey's expression hardens. "More protection than you deserve, considering what you were trying to do to that girl."

Claire sniffles, and my heart squeezes with what she's been through. With that in mind, I suddenly trust this asshole's information a lot less.

"Grey," I say quietly, hugging my hands to my arms. His gaze snaps to mine. I glance back at the girl still cowering in the corner. "Can we go?"

"Yeah," he says with a sharp nod. "This was a waste of time. Sorry for dragging you out—"

"Shit. She tells you to jump, and you're already asking how high." Trucker snickers. "Looks like you finally went and got yourself a real boss to run this shitshow."

Grey glares at him. "You already got more than you deserve from me tonight."

Trucker's lip curls as he looks at me again. "You've already gone to their side." He clucks his tongue. "A damn shame too. Your old man would've welcomed you with open arms. You could have been on the winning side of this fucking war right along with the rest of us. But now... you're fucking worthless to him. The only thing you're good for is securing me my rightful fucking seat at his table."

A ripple of unease runs through me. How can I secure his seat with Franco?

Before I can ask, he springs to his feet. My shock sends me reeling backward as he transforms into a wolf and lunges—not at Grey but at me.

"Run!" Grey's command is swallowed by the attacking wolf's snarl that echoes off the concrete.

I turn and race for the door then veer toward the wall to avoid getting tackled as the angry wolf attempts to head me off.

Grey's friends surround me and Claire, shoving us back against the wall and screaming at us to get out. I make sure Claire goes first and then stumble sideways to avoid getting smashed.

On the far side of the room, Grey shifts, his human body transforming into an enormous wolf in less than a blink. The sight of it distracts me, and I barely avoid getting cut to ribbons by Trucker's claws before I'm yanked out of the way just in time. But the angry wolf is already coming again, and Grey's snapping teeth are barely holding him back.

In the next second, whoever's holding my arm releases his grip, and I tumble toward the floor, knowing with startling clarity that it won't be fast enough or far enough to avoid the attack that's coming.

Behind me, someone yells, and then, as my body slams into the concrete floor, an ear-splitting howl rings out and then goes abruptly silent. I wince, curling into a ball on the cold floor as I wait for sharp teeth to sink into my flesh.

Instead, hands grasp my shoulders, and I snap, swinging out and thrashing against my attacker.

"Whoa."

Through my hair covering my eyes, I see Grey's lanky friend trying to help me up. I shove him back, scratching at his wrists until he gives up and backs away.

Then, Grey is there, dressed in nothing but a pair of shorts, reaching down and pulling me up with an iron grip that no amount of fighting will loosen. He crushes me to his chest in an embrace that feels a lot like relief.

"You okay?" he asks, the words still muffled in my ears.

I don't answer.

"Did he hurt you?" he presses, releasing me far enough to look into my eyes.

I glare up at him, fear and shock and confusion whirling into a rage that has me balling up my fists and preparing to aim them at his face. It's so much—Claire and Trucker and the wolf and nearly being killed. I can't process it fast enough, and nothing makes sense.

Grey watches me with enough worry to make me believe he actually cares about whether I live or die—but that's wrong. It has to be wrong.

Nothing about this night is right.

Then he moves, and I catch sight of the body on the floor beside him.

The man—Trucker—is back in human form. Naked, facedown, and coated in his own blood. If there's a wound, I can't even see it through the layers of blood and grime.

My stomach rolls, and I look away.

That man died tonight... because he tried to kill me. Grey killed him to protect me.

My confusion wins out just as a warm hand lands on my shoulder.

"Lexi." Grey's voice is gentle, but after the point-blank murder he just committed, I don't care how nice he talks to me.

I don't care about him at all.

He was protecting me. But it doesn't change what he did. Who he is.

Does it?

The confusion pisses me off, and I'm left with only my anger to protect me. So, I use it. I funnel it all into hating the man whose fault it is I'm here at all.

"Take me away from here," I demand. "Take us," I correct icily, glancing back at Claire, who is trembling while silent tears track down her cheeks.

She looks like I feel.

I grab her hand and pull her close.

Her skin is cold, but she doesn't fight me holding onto her. If anything, she tucks herself in tighter against me.

Grey looks from her to me and nods then leads us out of the room. His friends part to let us pass. No one speaks though they cast me heavy looks that I resolutely ignore.

Fuck them.

Fuck this whole crazy-ass city full of violence.

The guy who met us at the door earlier follows us back out again. The other two stay behind, and I refuse to let myself think about what they'll do with Trucker's body.

At the exit, Grey stops long enough to tell his friend, "Clean this up, and come by when you're done."

"And your dad?"

Grey frowns. "What if I said it's none of his business."

The guy shrugs. "Then it's not."

Grey nods. "See you soon."

"You got it, boss."

"Don't call me that." Grey snaps.

The guy smirks then turns and disappears back inside.

Still scowling, Grey unlocks the car and opens the back passenger door. Ushering Claire in first, I slide in behind her.

Grey closes the door behind us, but I don't speak. Not even when he climbs in behind the wheel and turns the car on, blasting the heat and aiming the vents at Claire shivering beside me. I can't bring myself to acknowledge his gentlemanly gesture. There's nothing gentle about him, no matter how much he pretends. He's a killer and a kidnapper and a mafia prince. I can't let myself forget that ever again. Even if he just chose to save me rather than throw me to the wolves.

14

LEXI

*C*laire doesn't speak on the ride back into the city. I hold her hand in mine, noting how cold she is, but even then, she doesn't say a word. I bite my lip, debating whether to press her for answers, but my mind is too busy demanding answers of my own. Rather than replay the scene in that warehouse, I focus on the fact that these men are capable of shifting into wolves. And, if Grey's claims about me are true, so am I. It's terrifying to think about, but I can't help wishing for it anyway. If I were a wolf, I could fight my way free. But it's not like I can ask my captor for answers when giving them would mean giving me the upper hand.

Grey pulls to the curb out front of a fancy high-rise apartment building, not unlike his own.

"Where are we?" I ask.

"Meeting a friend." Grey's eyes flick to Claire in the rearview. "Someone who can help her get home."

"Home?" I shake my head. "She needs a hospital."

His gaze snaps to mine. "That's not how it's done."

"Well, where I'm from, when a girl's attacked, she deserves—"

"What?" he snaps, eyes shooting daggers at me. "Justice? Isn't that what she just got?"

I hesitate. "Medical attention," I say, my tone icy.

"She'll have what she needs," he says cryptically, and I follow the direction of his glance through the window where a figure peels off from the shadows and approaches the car.

I tense as the figure bends and opens Claire's car door. A woman, not much older than me, with riotous red hair peers in at us. She tosses Grey a shirt that he quickly pulls on. Then she looks at us in the backseat.

Beside me, Claire grabs my arm with her free hand, clinging tightly.

"What—" I begin, alarmed.

"Relax. This is Mia. She's going to help." He turns back to look at Claire pressed against his backseat. "Mia is Reyes' daughter. She's part of my squad, and she's going to keep you safe," he tells her. "Okay?"

Mia doesn't say a word as she waits with the door held open. She flicks a curious glance at me but otherwise seems as if this whole thing is just another Tuesday night. Maybe for her, it is.

My earlier resolve to see this girl to the hospital is slipping away. Something about the smooth transition he's offering tells me this isn't the first late-night rescue he's made in this city, and the idea of it throws me off balance. Suddenly, he's not the evil I'm fighting against.

Just like he's not the one to blame for what happened at the warehouse.

Before I can think of a reason to stop her, Claire whispers, "Okay," and slides out of the car to join Mia on the sidewalk. She looks over her shoulder at me and says, "Thanks."

"Sure," I mumble as Mia shuts the door.

On the sidewalk, Mia wraps an arm around her and whisks her into the front door of the apartment building.

When they're gone, I face forward again and find Grey watching me from the rearview mirror.

"Want to come up front?" he asks.

I shake my head, and he peels smoothly away from the curb without another word. The entire drive back is a mental tug of war with myself as I try to reconcile the two halves of the man before me. He's twisted enough to kidnap me and drop me into the middle of a war, and yet tonight, when he could have stepped aside and let me die, he saved me. And then he saved Claire.

At least, I assume that's what the Mia woman will do.

I still have no idea who the good guys are here. So far, no one's proven themselves good. It's more like opposing forces of evil trying to one-up each other on just how corrupt they can be.

Back in the penthouse, Grey drops his car keys onto a tray by the door. My eyes track the motion—not that it matters since there's no way out of here for me—as the elevator door seals shut behind us.

Despite the softness of the sound, there's a finality to it.

I begin to tremble.

"That shouldn't have happened," Grey says to me.

I turn, struggling to keep my emotions in check. "No," I agree, "It shouldn't have."

The trembling only gets worse as he steps closer to me. I try to call up my earlier anger. It's so much easier to hate him than to let him see my fear.

But his hard expression has lost its granite coating. Now, I can see the exhaustion hovering behind his dark gaze. "If I thought for a second..." He runs a hand through his tousled hair. I wonder what it would feel like if I did the same thing. Burying my hands in his hair, arms wrapped around his broad shoulders, mouth—

"I never would have brought you in there if I knew he was going to come after you like that."

"Right. Because you're so worried about my safety." I snort and turn for the hallway so he won't see how distracted I am.

"I fucking saved your ass tonight," he snaps, and I stiffen. "So, yeah, I think we can both agree your safety matters to me."

I turn back, my eyes narrowing. "You kidnapped me, injected me with drugs, and brought me into a city where half the population wants to kill me simply based on which family I was born into. A family I never knew existed before you dropped me into the middle of this shitstorm. Without you, I could have lived my entire life in blissful ignorance, so if you're looking for gratitude, you're not going to find it with me."

"I told you—"

"And on top of ruining my life as I knew it, you walked me into some kind of gang execution tonight and made me watch you kill a man at point-blank range. You'll have to excuse me if I don't believe you consider my safety a priority."

"He was going to hurt you," he says, his voice dipping dangerously low.

He's pissed.

Join the club, buddy.

"You mean like *you* hurt me," I retort.

His eyes flash, and he stalks closer until he's standing right in front of me. I force myself to remain where I am even though everything in me wants to back away, to get a little more breathing room. To remind myself how much I'm supposed to hate the idea of him backing me against this wall and touching me until I lose all common sense.

"I have done nothing but protect you from the moment we met," he says.

"Bullshit," I snap.

His voice rises as he says, "I protected you from Trucker tonight, whether you choose to believe that or not. Hell, I even protected you from my own father—"

"And who's going to protect me from you?"

His gaze is dark, the storm in his eyes full of thunder crashing. "I'm not going to hurt you, Lexi."

"You already have."

The words are out before I can stop them. It's the most honest, vulnerable thing I've said, and I hate that I've let it slip.

"This is about the lap dance." The anger melts away, and in its place is a predatory sort of triumph that makes my skin heat. I'd rather have the anger. At least then, I'd have some semblance of control over this thing between us.

"That dance didn't mean shit," I lie.

I'd fold my arms over my chest, but he's standing so close my forearm brushes his shirt.

Dammit.

When did he get this close?

I drop my arms again, fisting my hands at my sides as I struggle to breathe, but every inhale is full of him.

He cocks his head. "Didn't it?"

Even as I hate myself for it, I can feel a flush creeping into my cheeks. "Why did you make me do it?" I whisper.

He glances at my mouth then back up again. "I didn't make you do anything."

My back hits the wall. I didn't even realize I'd retreated, but it doesn't matter because he's crowding in already, stealing all the oxygen between us. All the power and control. Just like that first night. I'm helpless to stop him. To stop falling.

"You know what I mean," I say, breathless because I refuse to breathe him in anymore.

He studies me, and I bite my lip, every nerve ending in my body tuned to him now. His head dips lower, and in that moment, I know he's going to kiss me. And damn if I don't actually want him to.

But I can't let myself fall into the same trap I did that first night.

Not again.

Not when he's used it against me every step of the way.

So, I steel myself against how badly I want him and wait.

The moment his lips brush over mine, I allow myself a shudder of pleasure, and then I whisper against his mouth, "I'll agree to your father's terms on one condition."

He pulls away, and I ignore how much I hate his retreat.

His eyes blaze down at me before his careful mask slips into place.

"And what is that?"

"I want a meeting with my grandfather. In person."

He frowns. "Meeting Franco's a bad idea. Especially after tonight."

"You seem pretty good at bad ideas to me."

He scowls. "I'm serious, Lexi. Trucker clearly had orders to kill you. Who the hell do you think it came from?"

"I don't care. Give me that meeting, and I'll pretend whatever you want. Engagement, marriage, whatever. When it's over, I walk away, and you can sit on your little mafia throne in peace."

He steps back, dark gaze flashing with something that looks like disappointment. "You think that's what I care about?"

"I have no idea what you care about, but I know it's not me."

"Lexi." He exhales. "That lap dance... I've never done that before."

"That makes two of us."

He nods, wincing. "I know."

"Right, I forgot. You stalked me beforehand. Had to make sure I was vulnerable enough to fall for your tricks."

"No, I— Fuck, you're stubborn." He grips my upper arms. "Haven't you wondered how it's possible that you're related to an alpha wolf shifter and yet you can't shift yourself?"

The question throws me off. It's not a jab I expect, but it's too logical to ignore.

"Maybe," I hedge, wary about why he's bringing this up now.

"Look, the reason I asked you for the dance was to sense your wolf, and I needed to be close to do that."

"There were other ways to get close," I snap.

"Maybe, but I shouldn't have had to get close. Most wolves can sense each other a mile away. Your wolf is barely noticeable from a distance, and I needed to know for sure. The lap dance isn't something I planned, but once it started…"

He shakes his head, his hands releasing my arms. Suddenly, I desperately want to know how that sentence ends.

"Once it started," I prompt.

He opens his mouth just as his phone rings.

Scowling, he slides his phone out of his pocket and steps back as he presses the phone to his ear.

"Yeah?"

He listens for a few seconds then says, "I'll buzz you up."

He ends the call and looks back at me.

"I'll see what I can do about a meeting," he says.

My heart squeezes. For reasons I can't even name, his agreement feels like a rejection. On top of that, he never finished his sentence, and I'm dying to know what he would have said. But I nod and simply say, "Thank you."

He starts for the elevator and the keypad beside it but then pauses and turns back.

"All this," he says, gesturing around us, "Bringing you here, playing their games, that was for duty. But the dance… Lexi, that was all for me."

15

GREY

*B*y the time the elevator opens to reveal a freshly-showered Dutch, Lexi has stomped off to her room. It's just as well. No good will come of her pushing me about that stupid fucking lap dance. The worst part is that I don't regret it, even though I know I should. I wasn't lying either. At the end of the day, she's right. I could have found another way to get close enough to sense her wolf, but I chose that stupid fucking dance. And I did it for one simple reason: I wanted her, even if for only a minute. The worst part is I actually thought a minute would be long enough.

Fuck.

"How'd cleanup go?" I ask Dutch as he steps off the elevator.

He goes straight to the fridge and takes out a beer. "You want one?" he asks.

I shake my head.

He shuts the fridge and crosses to the couch. Sinking onto the cushions with an audible sigh, he cracks the can and lifts it to his mouth for a long sip. When he's done, he says, "Razor and Crow are finishing up, but I stayed back long enough to make sure we were in the clear."

"Thanks. All I need is my old man hearing it from someone else that we carried out a sentencing without him."

He grunts because we both know I'm playing a dangerous game by not telling him what happened with Trucker tonight. A few years ago, I wouldn't have dared keep something like this from him, but my time away changed me.

Hopefully, it didn't make me stupid. Because if he finds out I put Trucker down without consulting him, there'll be hell to pay. I should worry about such a payment, too, but watching him go after Lexi like that...

I didn't think, I just acted.

Now, all I can do is minimize the fallout.

"How'd it go here?" Dutch asks.

His gaze flicks to the hall.

"Dropped the girl with Mia," I tell him.

"And your guest? How is she feeling about nearly getting her throat ripped out?"

I sigh as I sink into the chair beside him and lean my head back so I can stare up at the ceiling. There's a tiredness in me that has nothing to do with missing a night of sleep. "Fine."

"Doesn't sound very fine. Is Her Highness giving you trouble again?"

I snort and look back at him. "When is she not?"

He grins. "Babysitting duty not your speed, eh?"

"She wants a meeting with Franco," I say, running a

hand through my hair as I straighten. "In exchange, she'll play the part of doting fiancé."

The grin vanishes, and he whistles. "Gotta give it to her, she's got balls for wanting to be in the same room as that fucker."

"She's naïve," I snap. "She has no idea what she'd be walking into."

"So, tell her."

"I tried. She doesn't believe me."

"Or she doesn't care."

I glare at him. "Whose side are you on?"

"Yours, bro, but think about it. She has no family. No idea who she is to any of our kind. All she has is the word of a stranger and a prick who tried to kill her for her troubles. Makes sense she needs to hear it from Franco himself."

I glare at him. "What are you, her therapist?"

"I'm just saying that I can see her side. Besides, have you seen those legs of hers?" He winks. "I'll be whatever she wants if it gets me on her good side."

The hot stab of jealousy his words provoke is instant and guttural. I snarl, springing out of my chair when he throws both hands up and leans away.

"Whoa, the fuck." His eyes are wide until the moment I manage to force myself to ease back again. My breaths are heavy and quick, my heart pounding.

Dutch relaxes only to lean forward, eyes narrowing instead. "You want to tell me what the hell that was?"

I huff out a breath, nostrils still flaring at how hot my blood is pumping.

"I don't know," I say darkly. His brows lift, and I flip him off. "Stop looking at me like that."

"Stop acting like a jealous mate, and I'll stop looking at you like one."

"Now you're *trying* to rile me up."

"I'm trying to figure out why you just went ape shit over the princess." He speaks slowly, letting me know he's being serious rather than fucking with me some more. And that somehow makes it worse. "And there's still the matter of you going rogue tonight."

"Trucker had it coming."

"That may be, but we both know he didn't have it coming from you. Not until he went after *her*." He frowns. "What's really going on with you, man?"

I don't answer.

It's not that I don't trust Dutch. He'll have my back, no matter what. But what he's asking… I'm not ready to admit it to myself.

Avoiding his gaze, I get up and head for the fridge, changing my mind about having that drink. "Your guess is as good as mine."

The lie doesn't convince either one of us, but he lets it go.

My phone dings with a text that I ignore. A second later, my phone rings, but I ignore that too.

Dutch looks at me pointedly. "You gonna get that?"

"Nope." I crack my beer and take a swig.

Dutch just stares at me, clearly waiting.

"It's Ramsey," I say.

Dutch's brows lift. "You two feuding or something?"

"No. The opposite." I take another long drag of my beer.

The longer this day gets, the more I think alcohol is the answer. I drop back into my chair and look at Dutch, who is clearly waiting for an answer. "He's been calling nonstop since I got back. They all have."

"They missed you. What do you expect?"

"That's not it, and you know it."

"I don't know shit."

I glare at him. "You're a lying sack of balls."

He shakes his head. "Dude, you should talk to them. After you left… I know you can tell shit's different now than it was."

"We're all different," I toss back.

"The squad isn't the same frat boy party crew it used to be."

"You trying to tell me you, Ramsey, and Razor don't still burn it down?"

"Sure," he shoots me a grin I recognize all too well. That smile has led me into some dumb shit over the years. Just thinking about it makes me shake my head. "And Crow still picks us up when we've had too much, the little homebody. But we want more than booze and ass in our future, man. Ramsey's calling you because he knows you do too."

"That's the problem." Dutch starts to reply, but I cut him off. "I was only supposed to come back for this one last favor. Now, I'm dragged into the middle of his fucking war, which is what he wanted all along."

"You got anything better to do?"

He wants to see if I'll choose my other friends over him. I won't. My time with Levi taught me a lot. Training to be a soldier made me stronger and wiser. Less likely to rush into danger like I did the first time. But they aren't my pack, and even if I hadn't been dragged back here, they never would be.

Dutch is my pack. He knows it too.

"The Hills aren't all bad," he says when I don't answer. "And this place needs you more than you think."

I don't know how to respond to that, so instead, I drink until the can is empty and Dutch's words are no longer ringing in my ears.

When I've drained my beer, Dutch keeps watch, letting me catch a short nap, but even after I wake, Dutch informs me Lexi hasn't come out of her room once. For some reason, that only sours my mood further. I consider going to check on her, but my pride refuses to be the one to step onto her turf. Not that her bedroom—in my family's apartment, no less—is her turf, but it feels like giving in somehow, so I don't.

Instead, I take out my phone and use my family's private concierge app to order her some clothes. My father had promised to send some over, but I have a feeling it's not exactly high on his priority list. I consider calling Mia, but she'd only bitch at me for avoiding her calls, and that's not a conversation I want to have. I wasn't even sure she'd show up for Claire last night, considering how badly I've ghosted her, but Mia's not the type to take out her feelings on the innocent.

I sigh because that's exactly what the fuck I've been doing to Lexi.

Maybe getting her some clothes will help tip the scales somehow. The sizing questions throw me off until I'm reminded how little she wore during that dance, grinding her sexy body against mine. I never put my hands on her, but I can remember clear as fucking day what it felt like to have her pressed against me. Using the memory to pick out sizes and styles, I smile to myself. If some of these items are a little snug on her, I won't mind it at all.

When I'm finished, the delivery service replies almost instantly to my request, letting me know they'll have the order sent over within the day. I spent years avoiding this life and all the expectations that came with it, but for the first time in a long time, I appreciate the perks. Having clothes delivered means I'll get to see her face when she opens the packages, and the thought of making her even a little bit happy makes me want to grin like a fucking lunatic.

Grabbing the remote, I decide a distraction is in order. Anything to keep from wondering what the hell she's doing in that bedroom. And to keep from wanting to go find out for myself.

Mia texts me a few minutes later.

The girl's settled and safe. Her parents don't know.

I text her back, **thanks.**

A second later, my phone dings again. **Is *your* girl settled and safe?**

Me: **I'm not doing this with you.**

Mia: **You're being a bitch.**

Me: **So are you.**

Mia: **You'll pay for that.**

Me: **I'm not scared of you.**

Mia: **It's not me you should be worried about. Ramsey wants to know why you'll text me and not him.**

Groaning, I toss my phone aside and refuse to look at it again.

I'm halfway through an old James Bond movie when the elevator dings to signal a visitor. There's only one other person on the planet who can get past my guards out front, but I check to be sure. Grabbing my phone, I pull up the camera in the parking garage through my app and groan.

"Dutch," I say, tapping his shoulder as I push to my feet. "Wake up."

"Hmm?"

"Boss is here."

He sits up, instantly alert. "What's he doing here?"

"No idea. Go into my room, and make sure Lexi doesn't come out of hers until he's gone."

He gets to his feet. "Yeah, man. I got it."

I snag the empty beer cans and chuck them in the trash as Dutch slips down the hall and into my bedroom, closing the door behind him just as the elevator doors open and my father steps into the apartment.

"I'm starving, so this won't take long." He greets me with barely a glance.

"If you'd let me know you were coming, I could have had some food sent over—"

"No need." He waves a hand, striding past me into the living room and over to the floor-length windows that overlook the city. White, puffy clouds float by in a baby blue sky, but he doesn't look at the view. He only looks at his own reflection, smoothing his mustache before turning back to me.

"Well?" he demands. "Have you convinced the little bitch to see things our way?"

My hands twitch at my sides, wanting badly to clench into fists. But my dad's sharp eye misses nothing, and I force myself to chill the fuck out. She's not mine to protect, I remind myself.

"She agreed to go along with the engagement on the condition that we let her meet with Franco first."

He laughs humorlessly. "Absolutely fucking not."

"If it gets her—"

"She's in no position to make demands, least of all something completely fucking insane. Hell no."

"She has only our word that she is who we say she is," I tell him. "If she can hear it from Franco himself, I think it'll—"

He stalks over and gets in my face. "You think it'll what? Make her *feel better*?"

"It would be easier to have her cooperation in this," I say quietly.

"Cooperation?" he snaps. "Are you crazy? Have you been gone so long you forgot what it felt like to be played?"

"She's not playing me."

"And what about Franco, huh? You think, if we let her walk in to see him, he's going to let her walk out? That old fuck would sooner kill her than let her be used by me."

His words are truer than he knows, but I'm not about to tell him Franco's already tried taking her off the board once.

"We brought that girl all the way here to use against the old man, not to hand her over to him," he adds.

I should let it go. He's made his position clear, and he's not someone that changes his mind. Five years ago, I would have stopped here. But today, I push.

"I'd put countermeasures into place designed to remove

her when her time is up," I say. "She wouldn't remain in his custody."

"Bullshit," he snaps, stopping his pacing to glare at me. "You're talking about an outright battle right there in his fucking headquarters. He would see it as an act of war."

It's all I can do not to roll my eyes at that. "Kidnapping his granddaughter was already an act of war—"

"I've made my decision."

I turn away before he can see the fury in my eyes.

"Now," he says, his tone smoothing out and becoming way too calm, "what is this I hear about Trucker missing?"

I don't let myself react. "First I've heard of it."

"My sources tell me he was informing for Franco."

Swiveling back to face him again, I say, "So do mine."

"Any confirmation on that?"

"Not yet."

His eyes gleam, which is not at all how I expect him to be taking the news of a rat in our ranks. "Guess he did our job for us by telling Franco we had his princess."

I shrug and say, "Guess he did."

He scans the empty bar with suspicion. "You have any more trouble with the princess?"

"Nope."

His gaze flicks to the hallway toward Lexi's bedroom, and my heart thuds harder at the idea that he might go check on her himself. I ordered Dutch to make sure she didn't come out but didn't say anything about not letting my father in. Still, something tells me Dutch won't hesitate to step in front of that door if my old man comes that way.

It's not a confrontation I want though.

"She's quiet," he comments.

"Yeah."

"Got her ass tied up, eh?" he asks, arching a brow at me in amusement.

"She'll do what she's told," I say tightly.

He grunts in agreement at that.

"I better head out. Got a lunch meeting with the generals to talk about coordinating the next steps once your engagement is announced. You two be ready to go tomorrow night. I'll send a car."

The way he says the words—so casually—lets me know this fucked up engagement was his real plan all along. I'm just the last to know.

"Fine," I mutter.

He starts for the elevator, pushing the call button. The doors slide open, and he steps inside then turns to look back at me.

"And Grey? Don't fuck this up."

I don't answer as the doors close and he disappears.

When he's gone, I stalk over to the bar and pour myself a shot then immediately down it. The whiskey burns, but I welcome it against the rage crawling its way up my throat. One more minute, and I'd have unleashed it on the asshole.

From the hall, my bedroom door clicks open, and Dutch reappears.

His expression is wild, and I realize my mistake instantly.

"You cannot be fucking serious," he says. "That asshole expects you to marry her?"

"Keep your voice down."

He stares at me like I've just failed some test I didn't

know I was taking. Then, he steps back, shaking his head. "This whole thing is so fucked."

"No shit." I snort and pour myself another shot and one for him too.

He takes his, eyeing me over the rim. "You realize he's completely lost it, right?"

"Don't talk shit about the boss," I warn.

"My boss is standing right in front of me."

I groan. "Shut the fuck up, man. You can't talk like that."

"You already know it. I'm just saying it out loud."

"No."

"Then you're going to have to convince her to give her cooperation some other way," he says.

I stare back at him, my thoughts churning.

"Grey," he warns knowingly.

"Call Razor and Crow so we can go over logistics. If we're going to let her walk in and make sure she walks out again, we need a plan."

"Your dad—"

"Fuck him. She had one demand. Without it, I'm forcing her, and if I do that, no one's going to believe this marriage isn't real. Which means Franco's people will come for us, and then we're as likely to destroy the city and each other as win this war. I'm tired of watching him run us into the damn ground."

His eyes gleam because he wants this mutiny even more than I do. Before I can pull out of reach, he's clinking our shot glasses together and downing his whiskey. "I'll drink to that, boss."

16

LEXI

*A*fter watching Grey kill a man who was trying to kill me, then having him tell me that lap dance was his own personal bonus to the mission of kidnapping me, I'm convinced I won't sleep a wink. But the moment my head hits the pillow, I'm out like a light. For the next few hours, I stir occasionally at the sound of muted voices coming from the living room and even the ding of the elevator once or twice. Vaguely, I'm aware I should get up if only to keep my guard up and my wits about me while others are inside this apartment. But sleep manages to keep its grip tightly around me until, finally, I wake, groggy, starving, and unsure when I started feeling comfortable enough in this place to knock out for quite so long.

Padding into the bathroom, I'm reaching for the shower knobs when I suddenly remember I don't have a single shred of clothing to change into besides the slept-in, wrinkled, smelly ones I'm wearing and the even more smelly ones I arrived in.

"Fuck it," I mutter and peel off my clothes anyway.

If he refuses to buy me clothes, I'll go naked.

The shower is heavenly, the hot water doing wonders to wake me up and work out the kinks of the stress from the past few days. Time feels weird, like it should have been months since I was taken from the parking lot of Shady's and brought to a strange city where two feuding families are fighting over me like I'm their favorite toy.

Instead, it's been days.

And I'm already starting to adjust to this new reality.

For some reason, that leaves me disappointed in myself most of all.

I can't control what's been done to me, but the fact that I'm starting to lose my panic over it... it's wrong somehow.

When I'm done with my shower, I wring out my hair and wrap a towel around my body then grab my dirty clothes from the floor. Attempting to wash them in the tub doesn't help much, thanks to the stains left by the events of last night.

With a sigh, I give up on the idea of re-wearing them and instead yank my bedsheet off the mattress and wrap it around myself like a toga.

"Better than nothing," I mutter to myself and then march out before I can overthink my choice.

The living room is dimly lit by a cloudy sky that's threatening rain just outside the massive windows. After a quick glance revealing an empty room, I pad to the fridge in search of food. There's not much besides eggs and a takeout container of noodles I cannot be certain isn't spoiled. I do manage to find coffee and focus on making myself a cup before I commit to anything else.

The apartment is silent while I fumble with the

coffeemaker, adding grounds and water and hitting the power button. For a second, I think the place is empty and Grey left me here alone. It's not like I can get out, anyway, so maybe he—

The other bedroom door opens with a soft click.

A second later, Grey appears.

"Hey," he says.

"Hey."

His gaze rakes over my sheet-covered body, and I feel goosebumps rise along my skin at his perusal.

"What are you wearing?"

My cheeks flush. "I don't have any clean clothes."

Understanding lights his dark eyes; then his mouth quirks. "Actually, you do."

"What?"

"Come here."

He leads the way back down the hall. After a single second of hesitation, I hurry around the bar and follow him, stopping when he disappears into his own bedroom. Something about entering his personal space feels, well, personal.

"I didn't want to wake you up," he says from inside, "so I had everything brought in here for now."

Curiosity gets the better of me, and I follow the sound of his voice, passing through a bedroom done in muted grays and blacks and creams into a walk-in closet that's more empty than full.

On one side, I spot a selection of pants and shirts all similar to what he's wearing now along with at least half a dozen suits. On the other side, Grey is unzipping a garment bag and shrugging it open to reveal hangers full of women's blouses, shirts, dresses, and even a couple of evening gowns. There are six more garment bags next to the first one, each packed full.

"What is all this?" I ask.

"Clothes," he says simply.

I stare at him. "For me?"

"Of course. I told you last night that I'd get you more clothes."

"But…" He unzips another garment bag and strips it away to reveal more casual items. Sweatshirts, leggings, a tee that says "Meowdy" beneath a cat wearing a cowboy hat.

I snort and then look up to find him watching me. There's something about the way he's taking in my reaction that leaves me feeling exposed.

"Do you like it?" he asks.

"I—yeah. This is … a lot."

He shrugs. "I wasn't sure what you liked. What your style is."

I run my hand over the velvety gown in the first batch. "And you think this is my style?"

"My father says we'll be making the engagement announcement tomorrow night, and we'll need to look the part."

"I see." My stomach tightens with nerves. Suddenly, the simple gesture with the clothes feels more strategic than kind. "And did he agree to the meeting with Franco?"

"Yes. We're setting it up for tomorrow morning."

My eyes widen as surprise spears through me. I didn't expect him to go for it, honestly. But I smooth my features and nod calmly. "Great."

"May I offer a suggestion?"

"Sure."

"Go with the pants suit." He grabs a hanger off the rack of the first batch of items.

My brows lift as I survey its pinstriped pattern and classy, business-casual vibe. "Not really my style," I say.

"I meant for tomorrow. It's what Franco will respond to."

"I see. Um, thanks."

"I'll carry these over to your room if you're ready."

"Sure. Thanks."

I grab a garment bag off the rack to help him and nearly drop it from the sheer weight of the thing. "Holy shit, what's in this one? Bricks?"

He smirks. "Shoes and accessories, probably. They pack everything in garment bags rather than boxes. Easier to carry."

"Huh." I put that one back and select another, lighter option then follow him to my room, the ends of my sheet trailing behind me. "Who's they?"

"What?"

"You said 'they' pack in garment bags."

"Oh, right. The delivery service."

I wait while he hangs everything in my closet. "You ordered all this from a delivery service?"

"Yes. It was faster than shopping for it in person."

I stare at him, trying like hell to make sense of the man that is Grey Diavolo. One minute, he's killing a man in cold blood, and the next, he's ordering me cat t-shirts with funny sayings on them.

"What?" he asks and I realize I've been staring too long.

"Trying to figure you out, I guess."

He snorts. "Don't hurt yourself."

"Funny."

But he doesn't smile. If anything, he looks confused. "What's to figure out? I'm not that complicated."

"Yeah," I scoff. "Right."

"Okay then." He crosses his arms, challenging me. "What's so hard to understand?"

"You're a kidnapper, a killer, and a mafia boss's son," I say, ticking them off on my fingers.

"Is that all?" he shoots back.

"No. That's the problem," I say, shaking my head. "You're also a cook, a protector of young girls, and apparently a fan of punny t-shirts."

His lips twitch. "Is that last one a point for me or against me?"

"I haven't decided yet."

"Fair." His gaze holds mine, and the silence between us stretches.

"Is Grey even your real name?" I finally blurt.

Surprise flickers in his eyes and I can't help the disappointment that spears through me to realize it's not. "It's my middle name. When I left, I started using it as an alias."

"Left where?"

He hesitates. "I left the city for a few years."

"Where did you go?"

His expression tightens, and I realize too late I've crossed a boundary somehow.

"Away," he says simply.

"And now you're back," I say, trying to get us back onto even footing.

"For now."

I wait, but he doesn't say more. Instead, he stares at me with a look of such intensity I can feel it all the way through to my bones. Instantly, I go from trying to understand the contradictions he contains to losing myself in the dark depths of his eyes. He flicks a glance at my mouth, and I realize suddenly that we've somehow ended up in my bedroom with me in nothing but a bedsheet. And all I can think about is what he told me earlier, about how that lap dance was all for him.

In this moment, I'd dance for him all over again if he asked me to.

But he doesn't.

Finally, he looks away from me, toward the door at my back—like he wants nothing more than to escape this moment. An instant later, after a mumbled comment about grabbing the rest of my stuff, escape is exactly what he does, leaving me alone to catch my breath and add another contradiction to the list.

My attraction to Grey makes zero sense whatsoever, but it's only getting stronger the harder I fight it. The question is, what happens when I can't fight it anymore? Who will he be then?

17

LEXI

I force myself to take a deep breath and concentrate on steadying my nerves. From the window of the second-floor high-rise office where I stand in heels and a pantsuit more expensive than I used to make in a month, I stare across the street below at Altobello's Italian restaurant. It's a bit out of place among the surrounding skyscrapers with its one-story stature and red, checkered awning with cute little flower hanging boxes beneath the windows.

If I didn't know it doubled as the headquarters for a wolf pack mafia, I'd find it inviting. Instead, my stomach churns with nausea, and my palms sweat as I study the restaurant's tempered glass windows like they're the crystal ball I need to see how this will all play out.

"You ready?"

Grey's voice snaps me back to the present. I turn from the window and face him, nodding even though I'm pretty sure I might vomit at any moment. He frowns, studying me in a way that lets me know I don't have him fooled.

"Breathe," he says quietly.

"I am," I snap, mostly because, if he's nice to me now, I'll lose it. Especially since he hasn't spoken a word to me since our strangely friendly conversation last night where he bought me an entire wardrobe and then stalked out like I'd somehow offended him by repaying him with conversation.

His hot-then-cold attitudes are giving me whiplash.

At my snapping reply, he says curtly, "Let's go."

I follow him out of the empty office and into the lobby where a bank of elevators awaits us. The floor we're on is emptied of employees, and I can't help but wonder if it's some holiday I don't know about that's kept everyone away or if Grey orchestrated it so his men would have a clear vantage point. Men I recognize from the warehouse the other night though none of us mention it.

"This building is neutral territory," Grey says even though he already gave me this exact spiel on the drive over today. "We use it for meeting with lawyers and contract negotiations. When you get there, tell them my father brought you in here to discuss your prenup and you managed to slip away."

"How do you know Franco will be there?" I ask.

"Unless he's sleeping or fucking, he's there." He snorts. "Actually, even then, he probably—"

"I got it." I wave a hand so he won't say more about my grandfather having sex. Ugh. "And where will you be?"

"Close," he says, his eyes gleaming with an intensity that makes me nervous about my plan. "They aren't just going to let you walk out when you're finished. They'll say it's for your own protection, but you're walking into a death trap."

"You don't know that," I say, but he cuts me off.

"Yeah, I do. You think my father locking you in a tower sucked?" He grunts. "Franco's going to put you in a basement and never let you—"

"Okay, you've made your point. You think this is a terrible idea. But since I'm doing it anyway, where will you be?"

His eyes glitter with the promise of his words. "You won't see me, princess, but I'll be close enough to see you. Remember what we talked about. You get yourself to the front door. I'll do the rest, okay?"

"Okay."

The vagueness of his plan would have bothered me if I'd been at all intending on seeing it through. I do my best to keep my true intentions off my face while he hits the elevator call button.

The silence between us feels heavy. Or maybe that's my conscience.

No, I remind myself.

This man kidnapped me and used me as leverage in his turf war. I have nothing to feel bad about in trying to escape him. So why does it bother me so much that I intend to betray him? And why do I hate that this is goodbye forever?

The elevator dings brightly as it arrives, and the doors slide open. I step inside, turning to face Grey while I wait for the doors to close again. His hands are shoved into his pockets, the look in his eyes a bit wild as he stares back at me.

"Watch your back in there, princess."

"I will."

I wonder if he and I could have been friends if our circumstances were different. *Doesn't matter*, I tell myself as the doors slide closed. The circumstances we're in make us enemies. It's as simple as that.

I set my shoulders as the elevator carries me off to a future that doesn't include Grey Diavolo.

Out on the street, the traffic and noise threaten to overwhelm me. I've never been in a city this big. In another situation, it could have been fun to take it all in—the chaos and the fast pace of everything and everyone around me—but today, it's too much. My heart pounds as I move to the crosswalk and wait with the other pedestrians to cross the street. I don't look up at the office windows behind me, but I don't have to; I can feel Grey watching me anyway.

He's right. I won't see him, but I know he sees me.

For now.

The walk light turns green, and I move forward with the people around me. On the far side of the street, they turn left and right, the small crowd dispersing as they make their way quickly toward their destination.

I continue straight ahead until I come to stand beneath the red-checkered awning. Before I can second-guess myself, I reach for the door and push my way inside.

The lighting is dim, and it takes a moment for my eyes to adjust. As they do, I inhale the scent of Italian cooking. My stomach grumbles for it, but I shove that aside and scan the dining room. It's empty, but there's a coffee mug and ashtray sitting out on the table in the back.

I start toward it, but movement behind the bar startles me.

"You looking for a table?"

A man stands behind the mahogany bar, polishing a glass with a rag. He's older than me by a couple of decades with shaggy hair and stubble. There's a hardness in his eyes that has me stopping where I am.

"I'm looking for Franco," I say.

His stare intensifies. "What do you want with Franco?"

"I'm his—"

"I know who you are."

That startles me into silence. If he knows, then why is he giving me the run-around?

"Bobby," a male voice calls out.

A door at the back of the restaurant swings open, and a man not much older than me walks out. He's broad-shouldered and dressed in a suit that looks more expensive than anything I could ever hope to own. The way he walks, with confidence edging straight into conceit, cancels out the fact that he's mildly handsome.

"Pop said he wants you to—"

The newcomer stops when he catches sight of me, his brown eyes narrowing. "What the fuck do you want?"

I tense. This is not the welcome I expected. And I'm running out of time.

"I want to talk to Franco," I say in what I hope is a tone that is not to be fucked with. "Now."

The suited stranger scowls but turns around and yells through the swinging door, "Yo, pops. The little pole-dancing princess is here."

I clamp down on my tongue before I can snap back some snide reply about his choice of nickname for me. Already, I can feel the bartender's eyes glued to me in a way that has my nerves dancing on edge. Message delivered, the suit stalks toward me. His open suit jacket moves as he walks, and I glimpse a pistol tucked at his hip.

My body tenses as he gets closer, but I keep my chin high, refusing to let him see me squirm.

"You got some fucking nerve, walking in here like you're some prodigal coming home," he says to me.

"I'm here because I was kidnapped by the Diavolo family," I say.

His brows lift. "You trying to tell me you escaped Vincenzo Diavolo?"

"Yes."

He snorts. "Bullshit." He glances back at the bartender. "It's a fucking trap. Post up at all exits and call for backup."

The bartender sets the glass and rag aside and pulls out a phone then promptly starts texting. So much for Grey's exit strategy. Before walking in here, I was convinced I wouldn't need his help, but now I'm not so sure.

The suited stranger turns back to me, but his next words are cut off by another man stepping through the swinging doors. His hair is gray, and his dress shirt is wrinkled and coming untucked. A gold watch gleams from his wrist, and a thick gold chain wraps around his neck, sparkling beneath the restaurant lights. He looks more suited to car sales than running a mafia, but I've heard enough about what he's capable of not to underestimate him just yet. Besides, it's his sharp eyes that strike me now —they don't miss a thing.

"What is it, Dom?" he says as he strides toward us. His expression changes at the sight of me, though it's not exactly friendly. More like cold and closed off. "Well—well, what do we have? A special visitor."

I glance pointedly at the suited asshole—Dom, apparently. He doesn't move. "I'd hoped we could speak alone."

"You can say anything you have to say in front of Dom."

I ignore the smug look Dom tosses my way and focus instead on the older man, who is supposedly my grandfather.

"You're Franco Giovanni?" I ask.

"I am. How can I help you?"

I flinch. "I'm Lexi—"

"I know who you are."

"Then you know why I'm here."

"Actually, I have no idea why you've turned up on my doorstep."

"I was across the street for contract negotiations, and I escaped."

"Is that what he told you to say?"

My hands flutter at that. "I don't know what you're talking about."

His brows lift. "You're a terrible liar."

"I'm not—"

"My informants tell me you are betrothed to my enemy. Willingly. Do you not realize that makes you my enemy now too?"

"I never agreed to the marriage," I say. "It was forced on me. Vincenzo Diavolo plans to attack you. He's trying to use me in his war against you, but I refused."

"Is that so?" He looks me up and down, clearly unconvinced. "What exactly do you expect me to do about it?"

My temper sparks at that, and my eyes narrow. "I don't know. Maybe something more decent than having my parents killed and washing your hands of your only grand-daughter."

His eyes flash at that, but I keep going, too pissed to care what he thinks. "Or maybe I expected you to actually give a shit about me. To take me in when I had no one else instead of letting me grow up in shitty foster homes where I had to fight to survive."

His voice is hard and cold as he says, "Why would I take in someone who is nothing to me?"

My eyes widen, and despite what everyone has tried to tell me about this man, I can't help but feel shocked at his callous disregard. "I'm your granddaughter."

"You are your mother's daughter, that's clear to see."

"What does that even mean?"

"Tell me, can you access your wolf, or are you still merely a human weakling?"

"What do you know about my wolf?" I demand.

"I know you can't shift," he says, sniffing like he finds the idea of it below him.

"And that's somehow my fault?"

"No, your mother's the one whose genes are to blame for this error."

"How do you know?" I ask. "Was she not a wolf too?"

"She was. But her line wasn't proven."

"Proven?"

His expression tightens with impatience, but his voice remains the same even tone as before. If not for the hatred in his eyes, I would think him devoid of any feeling at all. "The Giovanni family line is filled with nothing but powerful alphas. This failure had to be hers."

Frustration and impatience bubble up in me. "Who

cares? You're treating me like I'm somehow the bad guy in all this when it's your turf war that dragged me down here in the first place. All I ever wanted was a family, but if this is what it's like to be related to you, I don't want any part of it. You and your little suited soldiers can all go to hell."

When I'm done, the room is completely silent. I know going off on him has only made him more likely to toss me out again, but I can't bring myself to grovel, either. Not after meeting him face to face and witnessing for myself his lack of remorse or caring about what he did to me or to his own child.

A noise outside cuts through the silence, and Franco's gaze whips toward the door.

"Boss," Dom says.

"Put her in the storage cellar," Franco says dismissively.

Panic spears through me. "What?"

Dom comes forward, but I shrink back before he can grab me.

"I came here to join you willingly," I tell Franco. "Not to become your prisoner."

"You clearly know nothing about our way of life," Franco says. "You can't simply walk in off the street and join an organization like ours."

"I'm your blood," I snap, "Doesn't that mean anything to you?"

"Why do you think you're still breathing?" he shoots back.

Dom grabs my arms and starts pulling me toward the back of the restaurant. I struggle, glaring at Franco, who's already turned his back on me and is headed for the back door too.

"You're just as bad as Vincenzo," I scream.

"Actually," Dom whispers in my ear, his tone gleefully cruel, "we're way fucking worse."

"You can't just lock me up," I protest, fear snaking down my spine as Dom drags me toward the swinging doors where Franco just disappeared.

He's way stronger than me, which means the fact that we're going this slow is his choice. He probably enjoys dragging it out.

"Oh, I plan to do a hell of a lot more than lock you up," Dom murmurs. "By the time we're done, Vincenzo and his little bitch son will know better than to fuck with us."

18

GREY

*T*he first explosion is a doozy. The force of it demolishes the asphalt road and concrete sidewalk and sends chunks of each hurtling in every direction. Car alarms sound, and screams ring out. It's fucking chaos. Razor rigged it that way on my orders, but still—I wince at the damage done to the corner of the block thanks to the explosives that have just decimated everything in its radius. The moment the ground stops moving beneath my feet, I launch myself out of the alcove where I'd tucked myself and race down the alley toward the back door of Altobello's.

When the second explosion goes off, this one right out front of the restaurant, I try not to think about casualties. Razor and Crow had explicit orders to clear the area of civilians before setting off their toys. But I have no way of knowing if they were able to do so without alerting Franco's men to what was coming.

Now, all I can do is hope no innocent lives got caught

in the crosshairs. And get Lexi the fuck out. If I can't do that, it was all for nothing anyway.

I'm nearly to the door when tires screech into the alley behind me. A quick glance back reveals a familiar sedan and Dutch's wild-eyed form behind the wheel.

He whoops loudly enough that I can hear him over the rev of the engine. It's his version of a hyped-up battle cry, one he swears will intimidate the enemy even before we reach them. For me, silence is the best weapon, so I keep my mouth shut and my eyes open as I crash through the restaurant's back door.

Two strides in, my path is blocked by a scraggly-bearded asshole I know by reputation alone.

"Bobby Malone," I pause long enough to say before smashing my fist into his face.

He rears back but doesn't go down.

"Grey Diavolo," he snarls, spitting out a mix of saliva and blood.

Straightening, he comes at me with a look of pure murder in his eyes. Get in line, buddy.

My second punch lands in his ribs, and I'm rewarded with a loud crack as they split beneath my fist. I hit him once more so that he falls unmoving to the floor, then I move farther inside, my senses tuned to any movement. The kitchen door swings open and Franco himself walks through.

He stops at the sight of me, surprised into a moment of stillness. Then, he blinks and comes to his senses, skirting me as he pulls a gun from his waistband.

"Diavolo!" His eyes widen. "This goes against the rules

of engagement, you cocksucker. I'll have your balls for this!"

He fires off a wild shot that I easily duck, and then he's gone, disappearing through a side door that I've heard leads to a series of escape tunnels.

I let him go, but I'm aware that every second I don't chase him down and rip his throat out is another failure in the eyes of my father.

The kitchen door swings open again, and I see Lexi being dragged in by Dominic Albero, Franco's second-in-command. Not only is he reputed to be a deadly bastard in his own right, but the prick's known for hurting women and enjoying it. Seeing Lexi caught in his grasp, I've never wanted to kill him more.

At the sight of me, Dominic snarls and adjusts his hold on Lexi, grabbing a fistful of her hair and yanking her in front of him like a shield.

Fucking coward.

"Grey Diavolo, you comin' to rescue your damsel?" Dominic taunts.

"Let her go, and I'll do the same to you," I tell him.

"And if I don't?"

"Then, I'll kill you. And I'll enjoy every fucking second of it."

He laughs like this whole thing is a fucking game to him. "I'm shakin' in my boots."

I don't bother replying with words.

Shoving forward, I drop into a slide and sweep his legs out from under him. He loosens his grip on Lexi but not enough to keep her from going down with him. I throw my body between them, shoving him down long enough for her to scramble away.

"Dutch has a car out back," I tell her, gritting my teeth as I battle with Dom for the upper hand. I'm not stupid enough to think he's an easy mark like Bobby was. If he gets me on my ass, I'm done.

"What about you?" she asks, hesitating.

Her presence is a distraction, and Dom manages to land a sucker punch to my jaw that has me seeing stars. Another punch lands and then another. I stumble, nearly losing my balance.

Dom steps closer and shoves me down easily.

"Go!" I roar at her and then give all my attention to putting this fucker out.

Scrapping on the kitchen floor like a couple of teens isn't my best work, but I can't let him get anywhere near Lexi. She moves out of my line of sight, and I can only hope she listened to me and ran for the car. But so far, no tires have squealed to signal their departure.

Fuck.

We've got seconds left—a minute if we're lucky—until Franco's backup arrives. I'm no match for all his boys.

Something clangs behind me, my head turning out of reflex. Dom's hand snakes past my defenses and curls around my throat, squeezing hard enough to cut off my air.

I shove at him, angling his head up and away so that his neck is pulled taut. Something moves beside me, and I don't have time to react before a cast iron pan smashes into Dom's exposed temple.

He goes slack, completely out.

I look up at Lexi, who's breathing hard and dangling the pan from her hands.

"Thanks," I tell her.

She nods, eyes wide, and I jump up, taking the pan away from her and setting it aside.

"We need to go," I tell her, pulling her out the back door and into the backseat of Dutch's waiting car.

I land with Lexi beneath me on the seat. Dutch hits the gas before the door is fully closed behind us. I peel myself off Lexi and sit up, pulling her with me.

"Are you hurt?" I ask as Dutch speeds out of the alley and into traffic.

"No," she says, but I'm too intent on seeing for myself to pay her words any mind.

Grabbing her face in my hands, I pull her close and scan her body. Her hair is a tangled mess, and her eyes are wide, but she's otherwise unharmed from what I can see.

Something inside me unfurls.

I exhale.

"You're hurt," she accuses, and I'm about to disagree when she reaches up and gently presses her fingers to my cheek. The pain has me hissing and pulling away. "Sorry." She drops her hand.

"It's fine," I tell her.

"Uh, guys." Dutch slows the car. "We're actually not fine."

I look ahead to see a barricade of black SUVs blocking the road across all four lanes.

"Fuck," I mutter.

"Is that Franco's people?" Lexi asks, and the wobble in

her voice has me grabbing her and tucking her against me without a second thought.

I look over at her, my wolf raging at the sight of them threatening Lexi. "I'm not letting a single one of them touch you ever again," I tell her, aware my wolf is speaking for himself right now.

Lexi doesn't answer, and I yank my gaze from hers, focusing on breathing to get a grip on myself.

Dutch eyes me through the mirror. "Thoughts?"

His tone is casual as he keeps his foot on the gas and the car aimed straight for the barricade.

"Take the alley toward the bridge," I tell him.

"He'll have backup along Magnolia," Dutch warns me.

"So do we." With my free hand, I slide my phone out of my pocket and dial Razor.

"Yeah, boss."

Fuck. Of course he'd call me that right now. Dutch probably put him up to it. Acknowledging that title is all the squad needs to officially back me, but I can't let that happen.

"We're taking Magnolia," I tell him.

"We're ready for you."

"Casualties?" I ask, tensing at the answer.

"None that we counted," he says, and I exhale, relaxing.

"Good work," I tell him. "We're headed your way in about thirty seconds."

"We can't wait to party," he tosses back, and then we both end the call.

"He's ready," I tell Dutch.

"Hold onto your titties," Dutch says, gripping the wheel

as we speed closer and closer to the parked SUVs. "Because here we go!"

He hoots as he makes a hard left at the last possible second. Still, a few bullets fly and land against our bumper, and Lexi squeaks. I wrap her tightly against me and hold us both upright as Dutch makes a series of jerky turns that sends us whipping through alleyways and out into oncoming traffic a few blocks away.

The other drivers honk wildly as Dutch jerks the wheel left and right to keep from crashing head-first into the moving vehicles. Speeding parallel to us on the correct side of the road is another black SUV, but it doesn't get far before Razor appears and uses his bumper to shove it up onto the sidewalk. The SUV crashes into a fire hydrant, and water shoots up like a geyser, raining down behind us in thick droplets.

"Woo!" Dutch cries.

I shake my head at my friend and remain silent as we speed along. Dutch is the best driver I know. Best fighter too, but today, his skills behind the wheel are more important.

"Still headed for the river?" he asks.

"Yeah," I tell him.

"Let's do it." Dutch makes another turn, putting us on a side road with less traffic and, more importantly, no more of Franco's SUVs on our tail.

"We made it," I tell Lexi when I know the coast is clear.

I start to ease away from her, suddenly very aware that I'm close enough to smell the scent of shampoo in her hair. But she grabs my arms and presses them around her.

"Don't let go," she whispers quickly. "Not yet."

I do as she asks, reminding myself I'm merely a warm body. She's not trying to hold onto me personally. She's looking for anyone who will protect her from the danger. Before I can stop it, I wonder what it would be like to be the one she wanted. Not for what I can do for her but for who I am.

My body heats against hers, but I shove aside the need that comes with it. Now's not the time. And Lexi's not the girl.

We drive on, leaving the city behind and the violence along with it. Realistically, I know the only reason we escaped was because we had the element of surprise on our side. Never, in the history of our families feuding, has anyone brought the fight to Franco's doorstep. It's understood between the factions that there must be a boundary around the sanctity of "home."

Today, I broke that rule. And not for just anyone either. For *her.*

There'll be hell to pay for it later, but even so, I don't regret it for a second. Not if it means Lexi's safe. Why that matters to me more than the exact sort of street war I've been trying to prevent for decades is a question I'm not quite ready to answer just yet. But I'll have to face it soon. I won't have a choice when my father finds out what I've done—and who I did it for.

19

LEXI

We drive until the skyscrapers give way to suburbs and those eventually disappear too. Finally, surrounded by trees and country roads, Dutch turns left onto a winding gravel lane with a full canopy of leaves hanging overhead, casting us into shadow. Up front, Dutch sings along to some rap song on the radio, but next to me, Grey is silent.

He hasn't let go of me yet. Not since he tried and I asked him to please hang on a little longer. I know it's an illusion, this truce and protectiveness he's offering, but I need it.

I need to pretend he's my white knight just for a few minutes.

Franco's attempt to lock me up is still an open wound. More than that, it's his rejection that left me reeling. Like the ground beneath my feet is slipping, and I have nothing left to hold onto to keep from sliding right off the edge of the earth.

Nothing except Grey's arms around me.

I hate that I need him right now.

And I hate how safe I feel with him beside me.

At the end of the road is a large log-cabin-style house with a wide front porch and a glimpse of water peeking out from behind the hedges and trees that surround it. The front yard is shady and serene, which is the exact opposite of the chaos we left behind in the city. And even though it's peaceful, I can't help but be suspicious of what hides beneath the surface of this place.

Dutch parks in front of the massive house and gets out.

"Come on," Grey tells me, climbing out and holding the door open for me.

The moment his arms aren't holding me anymore, I feel exposed all over again, but I refuse to beg for more, so I steel myself and climb out of the car. Hugging my arms around myself, I set my expression to hopefully hide how shaken up I am.

"Where are we?" I ask.

"My family's summer cabin," he says. At my expression, he adds, "Don't worry. We're the only ones here."

I have no choice but to trust him, so when he turns to follow Dutch around the side of the house toward the back, I trail after them.

In the backyard, there's a patio area with pavers where five Adirondack chairs are set up in a circle with a fire pit set in the center of it all. Dutch heads there, but Grey hangs back.

"Go sit and relax. I'm going to get us some drinks," he says and hurries toward the house, leaving me alone with Dutch.

I sit on the edge of one of the chairs, as far away from Dutch as I can get, and stare out at the river that winds past the edge of the yard.

"Family sucks, sometimes, doesn't it?"

I whip my head up to look at Dutch, trying to read whether he's just being a dick, but he looks serious.

"Did yours also disown you and let you grow up without love or safety?" I ask.

"Actually, yeah."

I blink in surprise at his answer. "You're fucking with me," I say warily.

"I'm the son of a general, so, no, I'm not fucking with you."

"What's a general?" I ask.

"Vincenzo has his territory divided up among four men he calls his generals," Dutch explains. "They're like property managers except they manage people, and by manage I mean enforce, kill, and terrorize."

"At least, you had your dad. How does that compare to what I—"

"Remember the terrorize part of their job?" His brow lifts as he explains, "Let's just say my dad's a fucking pro in his field because he had me to practice on. I might have been raised by the asshole who made me, but there was no love or safety in it."

I start to say I'm sorry again but then change my mind. The last thing I want are apologies from strangers that don't change anything. I have a feeling Dutch feels the same way.

Instead, I ask, "How does Vincenzo have territory and generals? I thought Franco was the pack alpha."

"Franco's the high alpha over the entire mafia pack, which is made up of all of Indigo Hills. Vincenzo is the alpha of the Giovanni pack, which is a smaller group within the whole."

"There are multiple smaller packs that make up the big one?"

"Only two packs. Giovanni and Diavolo. We used to have four, but the other two were taken over."

"By Vincenzo?"

"One of them," he nods. "The other was Franco deciding they were gaining too much power, so he took them out."

"Why hasn't he done that with Vincenzo?"

"Truth? I don't think he perceives the old man as a real threat."

My brows lift at that, but he shrugs. "I get it. Vincenzo's spent his entire life trying to unseat Franco, and he's never come close until now. I don't think Franco respects him enough to worry much."

"His confidence will be his downfall," I say.

Dutch nods. "Pretty smart take for being so new to all this."

"So, it all comes down to these two packs fighting for control of one another?"

"More or less. But to fully understand the hierarchy, you have to remember that we're also an organization. Think of it like a business."

I huff a laugh. "Being a wolf is business?"

"Being mafia is," he says with a shrug. "We all work for someone, and we all help generate revenue for the branch we serve."

"Okay, so Franco is like the CEO, and Vincenzo is what? A branch manager?"

"Vincenzo is another CEO, but his company is smaller and owned by Franco's."

"So, one pack, multiple businesses?"

"And only one alpha who owns them all," he says.

"I see." I blow out a breath, realizing there's more to the hierarchy of these people than I thought. And Grey hasn't bothered to share any of it.

I blow out a breath, realizing now more than ever that I need a strategy for how the hell I'm going to survive this clusterfuck I'm in. Step one: Learn all I can about how the politics work.

"So, Franco has his own generals, too."

He nods. "And believe me, they're just as bad as he is."

"Yeah," I agree, thinking of Dom. He knew the moment I walked in there that Franco didn't want me. Like they talked about it ahead of time. Planned it, even. And rather than explain it to me up front, he sat back and watched the show. "I guess I feel less guilty for knocking his ass out then."

"Whoa, hold up. What did I miss?"

"Dom and Grey were fighting, and I wanted to help, so I grabbed the first thing I could find, which happened to be a cast iron pan—" he hoots with laughter "—and whacked Dom so hard he passed out."

"No shit? Not just a princess, eh?"

"I was never a princess."

"No, I can see that."

We share a friendlier silence, and I can't help but feel like Dutch has accepted me into his circle somehow. Then my thoughts return to what Dutch said about his father. "Are all of Vincenzo's generals like your father?"

He shrugs as Grey finally returns with two cans of beer and a Red Solo cup.

"Pretty much," Dutch says.

"Pretty much what?" Grey asks, handing over a beer.

Dutch pops the top. "Your dad's generals are pretty much all the same toxic pieces of shit."

Grey grunts an agreement and walks over, offering me the Solo cup.

"What is it?" I ask.

"Double shot of whiskey, clean."

My gaze flicks from the cup to him, and my brows lift. "It's barely noon."

"It's that kind of day."

He's right. It is.

I take the cup.

Grey retreats and takes a seat on the low wall bordering the far side of the patio. He cracks his beer and drinks deeply, and I catch myself staring at the way his throat moves as he gulps his drink. The hard edge of his jawline is mesmerizing. I imagine what it would feel like to run my finger across it and feel his stubbled skin against my own. My distraction is ruined by the sound of tires crunching over gravel out front, and panic grips me like a hand around my throat.

The morning's events come crashing back. Dom dragging me off. Bullets flying at our bumper. If they've found us out here, there's nowhere else to go except for the river, and I can't swim.

Shoving to my feet, I nearly drop the whiskey as I look back and forth between the two guys, noting how calm they look. "Someone's here."

"Relax," Grey says. "It's just Razor and Crow."

"Actually…." Dutch trails off, wincing at the glare Grey shoots him.

"You didn't," Grey says, his tone full of warning.

But Dutch is unfazed. "This meeting was going to happen eventually."

"What meeting?" I ask, still on edge at the idea of strangers even if they are friendly ones, but Grey's already headed around front, muttering curses.

Dutch answers for him. "Mia, Ramsey, Razor, and Crow. Aka the squad."

Mia. The girl from the other night who we handed Claire off to. Razor and Crow I know already, not that we've actually conversed, but Ramsey's a new one. Before I can ask what Dutch means by "the squad," car doors begin to slam shut, and the newcomers all round the corner of the house, headed this way.

Razor is at the front with Grey. They speak in low tones that are impossible to make out from this far away. Behind him, Crow walks alone, his head down, his hands stuffed into his hoodie pockets. Mia, the redhead, brings up the rear. She walks beside a guy I've never seen before with thick, muscled arms and short, cropped hair that gleams golden in the sunlight. His face is mostly hidden behind Aviator sunglasses, but his lips are fixed in a smirk that suggests he knows a secret.

Ramsey, I presume.

When they reach the circle of chairs where Dutch and I wait, Grey steps back to let them pass. Razor peels off toward the house, saying something about refreshments. Crow slides into the circle and takes a seat beside Dutch, slouching in his chair and pulling the hood up on his sweatshirt. Dark eyes peer back at me from beneath his head before he looks down again.

"Bro, epic fireworks earlier," Dutch tells him with a soft punch on the arm.

Crow snorts.

"Double Dutch," Mia greets, smacking the back of his head as she passes.

Dutch ducks and scowls at her, but she ignores him as she winds around the circle toward me. She perches on the edge of the chair on my right and offers her hand.

"Hi, we didn't get a chance for introductions the other night. Mia Reyes."

I shake her hand. "Lexi Ryall."

"Glad to have you with us," she says.

I don't bother pointing out I'm not really with them. Her gaze flicks to something over my shoulder, and I turn to see the golden-haired stranger coming up on my left.

"Well, hello there," he says, holding out his hand and smiling wide to reveal two rows of perfectly straight, white teeth set against tanned skin. He peels the glasses off his face long enough to flash me with green eyes that glimmer. He's handsome, though his charm says he knows it.

"I'm Ramsey Greco. Son of the second general, though I hope to be first in your heart."

Mia groans and shakes her head.

"Lexi," I say as I tentatively place my hand in his and attempt to shake.

He immediately brings my hand to his lips but stops, my hand hovering just below his mouth when Mia says, "Ram, what did we talk about?"

Her tone reminds me of a schoolteacher with a toddler, and Ramsey drops my hand with a guilty moan. "Ugh. But this—"

"What did I say?" Mia cuts in sharply.

"No douchebaggery before three p.m.," he recites.

"Exactly." Mia gives him a prim smile and winks at me.

I take my hand back, not sure what to think of them. If they're a couple, they have very relaxed boundaries.

Grey clears his throat, and all the attention shifts from me to where he stands at the mouth of the circle, arms crossed.

"Good to see you, boss," Ramsey says, settling back in his own chair on my left.

"Funny considering you weren't invited," Grey tells him darkly.

"Damn. Rude," Ramsey mutters, looking wounded.

Grey's expression only hardens. "Say what you came to say so we can move on from this."

"Refreshments, anyone?" Razor returns, sliding past Grey, who remains immovable. Clutched in his arms is a half-full bottle of expensive whiskey and a few cans of beer. A bag of chips dangles precariously from his fingers.

"Right here," Dutch says, taking the bottle and uncapping it.

"Did you get cups?" Mia asks though the annoyance in her tone says she knows the answer.

"Uh," Razor says, clearly at a loss.

"Don't need 'em," Dutch says and then tips the bottle back, drinking straight from it. He swallows and then hands it off to Crow, who does the same.

Up front, Grey clears his throat, and Razor quickly takes a seat behind Dutch on the wall's edge.

"Dutch," Grey prompts when no one speaks. "You want to tell me why the fuck you called this meeting behind my back?"

"Because you wouldn't agree to it, and it needed to happen," Dutch says as if that explains—and excuses—everything.

"I can't agree to planning a coup," Grey snaps.

I jerk my gaze to his. A coup?

"You sure she should be here for this conversation," Razor says, nodding at me.

Mia tries passing me the bottle of whiskey, but I shake my head, too caught up in the conversation.

"She's the reason we can't wait to have this conversation," Ramsey says, and I look over at him, surprised he's defending me considering he's just met me. But he merely takes the bottle Mia passes him and swigs generously.

"Vincenzo's going to be pissed," Razor says, but he's grinning wildly.

Crow snorts, eyes gleaming with glee. "Understatement."

"Maybe we can keep the full details from him a bit longer," Dutch says, looking up at Grey.

Ramsey shakes his head. "It took out half a block in the center of the city. We can't hide this." He slides a case from his pocket, opens it, and picks a thin cigar from inside, which he promptly lights.

"Trust me," Mia says firmly, "He already knows."

"He knows we went against him by letting Lexi meet with the old man," Dutch says. "But he doesn't know we're setting Grey up to take his place."

"Don't start with this shit again," Grey says.

"What are you going to do about it?" Razor challenges. "Leave again?"

"Bro," Dutch says, shaking his head.

Grey doesn't deny it, though.

I pull my knees up to my chest, feeling like an intruder amidst their heated conversation. The heavy scent of Ramsey's cigar fills my nostrils, mixing with the faint aroma of the expensive whiskey they're passing around.

Grey's expression has grown tighter and more closed off since the discussion began. I can tell he doesn't like what they're suggesting, but he doesn't order them to shut up, either.

Beside him, Dutch and Crow are both slouched and relaxed, as if they couldn't care less what Vincenzo knows or does about it. Beside me, Ramsey exudes confidence and determination while Razor's impulsive excitement is written plainly on his sharply angled face. Mia still sits straight, perched on the front edge of her chair. She drinks when the bottle comes around again, her piercing gaze fixed on Grey.

"You can't keep running from this," she says when the group falls silent.

I half-expect Grey to snap back at her. Instead, he runs

a hand through his dark, tousled hair, and his gaze shifts uncertainly between his companions.

"I've told you all before; I don't want any part in the family business. It's not the life I envisioned for myself."

Dutch looks up at him in solemn sincerity. "We understand, brother, you know we do. But you're the only one capable of leading us. You've got the brains and the heart to steer us in the right direction." Crow grunts an agreement at that. "And you've got the cool head to keep us from getting ourselves killed in the process."

Ramsey and Razor exchange a grin at the last part.

Mia's voice cuts through the air like a razor. "Look, you may not have chosen this life, but you're a part of it, like it or not. And you're a part of us. Even if you leave again when this is all over, we're not going anywhere. This city is ours to burn or to save."

"I told you before, all of you can come with me—"

"And we told you, this is our home, and we don't abandon our people," she says, her eyes flashing.

Grey doesn't answer.

"We need a leader who's willing to fight for us, protect us," she says. "Someone who can bring stability to this chaos and put the people of this city first. And that someone is you."

Ramsey smirks, a glint of mischief in his eyes. "Yeah, brother, just imagine all the power, the respect. You've got the chance to rule this city, to make it yours. Don't tell me that doesn't tempt you even a little."

Grey's gaze shifts from one face to another, each one filled with expectation and hope.

His eyes linger on mine like he's finally remembered me

still sitting here, an outsider in this tangled web of loyalty and danger.

He takes a deep breath and looks back at the others. "I left because I never asked for this fucked up life. I owe my family nothing. And honestly, I don't owe this city shit either. But I do have a responsibility to the people who've stood by my side all this time."

"Fuck yeah," Dutch mutters.

"And," he adds slowly as if his hesitance is melting away as he speaks the words, "If we don't help the people in this city, no one else will either."

He looks at me again, this time with more force behind his gaze. There's a flash of emotion behind the hardened mask he wears, something that stirs my blood and makes my heart race. Like somehow, I factor into this decision he's making.

"It has to be us," Mia says firmly, and he looks back at her.

"It has to be us," he echoes.

"Whoop," Dutch calls out.

"Hell yeah," Razor says, pumping a fist in the air.

A wave of relief washes over the others, and even I can't help but feel a sense of anticipation for what lies ahead. I'm still the new girl, trying to understand the intricacies of this world, but I don't miss how Grey's resolve strengthens before my eyes. A reluctant hero taking his place in a world he never wanted—but a world that needs him nonetheless.

The others push to their feet, crowding in to high-five Grey, and I rise too but only so I can slip away. The weight of their words lingers in my mind as I head down to the riverbank. I'm still too new to this life to fully understand what it is they've just committed to, but I know it has to do with taking on both Franco Giovanni *and* Vincenzo Diavolo—two mafia leaders instead of just the one. Which means this journey has only just begun, and I'm about to witness something extraordinary—Grey, the reluctant mafia prince, stepping up to embrace his destiny and take back his kingdom. And I can't shake the feeling that he's doing it for me.

20

GREY

*R*amsey and Razor celebrate with more shots. Crow and Dutch drift off to plan a supply run despite me insisting we aren't doing this with violence if we can help it. Mia remains behind, quietly contemplating —like I knew she would. That girl never says everything she's thinking. It's one of the things that makes her a formidable foe—and a valuable ally. She's so much more than people give her credit for; I'm finding that most women usually are. And when she turns that strategic brain on me, it fucking scares me more than I want to admit. The look in her eye has me bracing for whatever she says next.

"He knows what you did to Trucker," she says when we're alone.

"How do you know?" I ask, hoping she's wrong. But Mia never is.

"I just do."

"Will he use it?"

Stupid question. I already know he will. It's what I would do if I were in his shoes. Not that I'd ever be in his shoes.

She shrugs. "When it suits him."

"Fuck," I mutter, glancing past her to where Lexi sits by the water. The moment I see her, every doubt I have vanishes. I lied to them before. I'm not just doing this for them or even for the people of this city. I'm doing it for her, which makes me the biggest kind of idiot.

There's never been anyone more forbidden or more off-limits for me than Lexi Giovanni. There's never been anyone less worthy of going against my father over. Hell, I left town for five years rather than pick sides against him, and less than three days back in town, with Lexi by my side, I've just declared war on the man.

For her.

My wolf wants her, and my cock craves her. It's two against one.

I'm so fucked.

"She's not what I expected," Mia comments, and I whip my gaze back to hers, searching for some clue about what she means. Or what I've given away from my silent brooding.

"She's not like us," I tell her.

"You hate her for it."

I start to argue and stop. Hate is good. Hate is safe. I need to hate her more—for both our sakes. But Mia isn't letting it go.

"She doesn't deserve it, you know."

"What?"

"Your hate. She didn't ask for any of this."

"Neither did we."

"No, but we're here, playing the game. Willingly." She looks at me. "Most of us," she adds wryly.

"Don't start."

"I'm not mad at you for leaving," she says, and I arch my brow so she knows I see through her bullshit. "Fine. Not anymore," she amends. "Your time away seems to have settled you."

"It did," I agree.

Made me more capable of violence too. I don't tell her that part, though.

"We need that calmness now."

"You're calm."

"Nah, I'm like the eye of a tornado. Besides, Lexi would have never fallen for me like she did for your pretty face. It had to be you."

"You're saying I'm only in charge because of my face?"

"Absolutely not. You also have that whole brooding, sad vibe that makes girls want to save you."

"I knew I never should have come back here," I grumble.

"You had to repay that favor you owed," she reminds me, all teasing gone. And even though we both already know it's true, it helps to hear her say it—that I did the right thing by coming back when he called me.

"We're even now," I tell her quietly.

She nods. "You owe him nothing," she agrees, quoting me from earlier. "But what do you owe *her*?"

I glare at her. "I hate when you use logic against me."

She smiles. "I know."

I stare at Lexi again, knowing full well what Mia is talking about. She deserves better, but more than anything, she deserves a choice.

It's the right thing to do. But it's also terrifying because, if she doesn't choose me, I'll lose her forever. I'll gladly fight a war against Franco and my father, but I don't think I can take it if she doesn't choose me.

If I were her, I wouldn't choose me.

Not after everything I've done to her.

But if I meant my own words before, then I have to start putting the needs of the people above my own. Starting now, apparently.

"I'll be inside," Mia says, rising and squeezing my shoulder on her way into the house.

I wait until she's gone before heading for the riverbank. They're probably going to be all glued to the fucking window, but at least, if they're inside, I can pretend we have some privacy.

Lexi looks up as I approach.

She doesn't stand, so I take a seat in the grass beside her, careful not to get too close. Even so, she pulls her knees into her chest and wraps her arms around them in a protective stance. I can sense how nervous she gets around me, and I can't blame her, nor have I done much to counter it before now.

Fuck, this is awkward. Being a grumpy kidnapper was way easier than actually being nice.

After a minute, I look over, and she glances at me uncertainly.

"Is this the part where you tell me you'll kill me if I talk?" she asks.

"What?"

"You let me sit in on a meeting where you all planned a coup against your father and a war against Franco. I'm a threat to you now. I know too much."

I sigh. "I let you sit in because you deserve to know what I plan to do to Franco. He is your family."

"No," she says, looking out over the water. "He's not."

I nod. "You're right. He's never been there for you. In fact, he's a monster. They all are. Franco, my father—everyone in charge. All they care about is obtaining more power, and they don't care who they hurt to get it. It's why we're planning to stop them. And I think you want that too."

She looks back at me.

"I don't want any of this," she says. "I just want to go home."

"I can't do that," I say, guilt pressing on my chest. "If I take you back, someone else will come for you. And they won't—"

"Won't what?" she asks when I pause. "Be this nice to me?"

She snorts, and I don't bother defending myself.

"They won't find you useful if you're alive," I tell her quietly. "And they won't hesitate to hurt your friends to get to you, either."

Her head whips to mine. She looks like she wants to argue, but then she sighs. "What the hell do you want from me?"

"Marry me."

Her eyes widen. "What?"

"Or pretend to marry me," I amend. "Like my father asked. Go along with the engagement so that our families look united."

"But you said you're going to—"

"Stopping my father will take time. And I'm going to do my best to find a way to do it without violence, which means remaining compliant for as long as possible. And earning the support of both sides of this fight."

"How does a fake marriage help that exactly?"

"My father's supporters don't trust me. I've been gone too long. I need to win them back, and love stories tend to do that." I look away as I say the words, my gut twisting with each one.

"And Franco's people?" she asks.

I blow out a breath, relieved she's not calling me out on the L-word. "Even if he disowns you, you are his rightful heir, and there's nothing he can do about that. Your alliance with me—"

"Makes you the next alpha of his line," she finishes.

This time, I do meet her eyes, and the words fall out of my mouth way too easily as I say, "Or our children."

"Oh." She looks away but not before I see a flush creeping into her cheeks.

My wolf stirs, and I fight the urge to reach over and kiss every square inch of her blushing skin.

She's so fucking beautiful, even now when I can tell she's weighing her life in her hands. And I hate that I'm putting her through it at all, but I don't know another way to save her anymore.

At least, I'm giving her a choice.

"There's another option," I say, hating the words as I speak them.

"What is it?" she asks, hope leaping into her gaze.

"I'm friends with the Black Moon Pack."

"The Black Moon Pack?"

"It's a pack of wolves located in a small town called Blackstone, Virginia. Levi and his mate Mac are the alphas."

"I thought there could only be one alpha of a pack."

I smile ruefully as I remember my time living and fighting alongside Levi Wild and his pack of Romantics, as they called themselves. For a few years, we hid out at a compound we created, helping other shifters escape the ruthless control of an alpha who punished them for choosing their true mates rather than rejecting them as a show of strength.

I learned so much from Levi and am damn grateful for my time with him. But the more time I spend with Lexi here in Indigo Hills, the less I can see myself going back there. Still, she'd be safe with them. And that's what matters.

"So did everyone else for way too damn long," I tell her. "Times are finally changing, though. In fact, they're the second pair of alpha mates running their own pack now." At her curious expression I add, "Those are both stories for another day. Anyway, I spent some time with Levi before he became alpha. He's a good friend, and I know he'd protect you with his life."

"What are you saying?" she asks.

"You could go to them. They would take you in. Hide you. Keep you safe. You wouldn't have to be a part of this."

"How long would I have to stay there?"

"Until I'm successful."

"And if you aren't?"

I swallow against the lump in my throat and say, "Then you'd stay forever."

Her silence stretches, and fear grips me as I wait to see if she'll choose me or her freedom. Hiding won't be nearly as bad as it sounds. She'd have a life there, a good one. Maybe even discover her wolf. And then she'd be free to mate—

"I don't want to spend my life in hiding."

Her words rip me from the nightmare unfolding in my head.

"You aren't safe otherwise," I tell her.

"It's not me I'm worried about."

Alarm shoots through me—a hot streak of jealousy that stabs my insides to the point of pain. But then I remember. The girl. Violet. Another dancer at the club. They were friends.

"You're worried about Violet," I say.

She looks surprised. "How did you know about her? Oh." Her expression shutters. "Right. You stalked me."

I start to answer, but she cuts me off.

"Violet's not the only one I miss."

The jealousy stabs at me again. "Who else is there?"

"There's a shelter for runaway teens not far from the club. I spend a lot of time there. Spent," she corrects.

I frown, wondering how I missed that detail. "I didn't know."

168

She glances at me then back at the water. "Yeah, well, I missed a few days of visits leading up to...well, you."

"Why?" I ask, genuinely curious about her life. It's not something we've talked about, and I realize now that's my fault. I assumed I knew her just from watching her for two days and letting her grind herself against me once.

I'm an asshole.

"I know what it's like to be alone in the world," she says. "And I think it's important to be there for the kids who had it like me or even worse."

I stare at her, struck by how simple she makes it sound. Once upon a time, I felt that way too. Until dealing with my father overshadowed my compassion, and I ran. Just like one of those kids in the shelter.

"And you miss them?"

She rolls her eyes. "Don't make it sound so pathetic. I don't have a squad of friends who have my back, okay?"

"It's not pathetic," I tell her. "I think it's incredible."

She looks back at me, her gaze softening. When she bites her lip, I track the movement, wishing I could scrape my teeth along that exact spot. My senses pick up on her heart rate beginning to increase. My cock stirs.

"I was going to stay with him," she blurts, and I blink, realizing her thoughts are nowhere near the direction of my own.

Her heart continues to pound, and I realize it's from nerves, not lust.

Fuck, get it together, dude.

"With who?" I ask.

"Franco. At the meeting. I was going to choose his side and stay with him."

I nearly smile at that. This is what she's nervous about?

"I know," I tell her.

She sits back, surprised. "You did?"

I shrug. "It's what I would have done. And it wasn't a terrible plan—well, if Franco had been a decent guy, anyway."

"Yeah," she agrees. "Too bad he's a prick."

I snort. "Too bad."

She looks at me again, and my smile vanishes at the look she gives me. Her heart has calmed, but there's a sadness in her eyes that pulls at me. For the first time since taking her out of her life, I feel like an asshole for not understanding what she lost.

"I guess I'm in," she says.

"What?" My guilt swirls with Mia's words echoing from earlier: This girl doesn't deserve my hate. The problem is I never hated her at all.

"I'll marry you," she says, and my wolf is way too fucking thrilled to hear those words. "Or pretend to." She waves a hand. "You know what I mean. But I'm making another condition."

"What is it?" I ask, trying to hide the fact that I'll agree to just about anything to make her choose me.

"When this is all over, I get to go home."

I hesitate, and she narrows her eyes.

"If I help you become the leader of this city, that means Franco and your dad won't have any power anymore," she points out. "And that means no one will want to use me as a bargaining chip. We can pretend to get divorced or something. Come up with some story. I want your word."

I nod, ignoring the pain in my chest at the idea of her

walking away from me. "If I win this war, you'll be safe to go home."

She sticks her hand out. "Deal."

I shake her hand, my body heavy with the feeling that I've somehow promised away the only thing that will matter to me in the end.

21

LEXI

*I*t strikes me as I draw my hand out of Grey's that I'm now officially here as a willing participant. Well, not willing, exactly. I'm only here because I can't go home. But I've agreed to be more than a puppet, and that changes everything.

Or, at least, it feels like it's changed me. When did I go from loathing him to enjoying the way his large, warm hand feels in mine? Suddenly, nothing makes sense anymore, and I have the distinct urge to redefine where we stand.

"Grey," I begin, but he stops me.

"Are you hungry?"

"I... sure, I guess."

"Come inside with me."

"Why?"

"Because you're part of the squad now."

I look back at him, more confused than ever. Just because we're allies doesn't mean we're friends... right?

"What?" he asks when I don't answer.

"I don't know. You're being nice to me. It's weird."

His lips quirk. "Just trying to keep you on your toes. I'm going to see if Crow managed to cook us up something. Will you come?"

He stands and holds out a hand.

I take it warily and let him pull me to my feet. My skin tingles where he touches me, offering a jolt of lust and something else I can't name. I realize my body has made a fast leap from friends to wanting to pick up where we left off with that lap dance.

Not happening, I tell myself.

Allies is one thing.

But wanting more than that—wanting him—is a disaster waiting to happen. He's my kidnapper, for fuck's sake. And the future mafia boss of Indigo Hills if all goes well.

I cannot be falling for the bad guy to end all bad guys.

Absolutely fucking not.

When his hand lingers in mine, I don't pull away first.

Inside, Crow has made scrambled eggs, bacon, and biscuits. Everyone else is nearly done, but there's plenty of food left. I want to ask if they're expecting an army or if Crow always makes this much, but that would mean getting a word in edgewise. At Grey's insistence, I slide in and make a plate while their conversation swirls around me.

"Crow, you're killing me with this shit," Ramsey says around a mouthful of buttered biscuit. "Just open a restaurant already."

"Seriously," Razor says. "He's the best cook in this fucking city."

"Hey, my mom—" Ramsey begins.

"Yeah, your mom," Dutch says and throws a balled-up paper towel that hits Ramsey's cheek. "No one does it better than her."

"Ohhh," Razor says, laughing, as Ramsey stalks over and attempts to shove the paper towel into Dutch's mouth.

Their scuffle becomes a wrestling match that nearly takes out the kitchen island. I step back, leaning on the counter and tucking myself into the corner to keep from getting caught in the fallout. Mia shrieks and shoves them out the back door, fussing at them to stop destroying property with their immaturity. They act like a group who've been friends forever, and I can't help but feel outside of it all.

Grey stands back too, and I catch him watching me more than once. It makes my heart thud stupidly every time, which pisses me off as much as it lights me up.

I finish my plate of food and turn around to face the sink behind me, mostly to escape his stare. The sink is full of dishes and pans, and I don't think about it; I just turn on the faucet and start washing.

A minute later, Crow comes up beside me and says simply, "I'll dry."

I glance back to see Grey's gone and Crow and I are the only ones left.

"Okay," I tell him.

He takes the clean plate out of my hands and goes to work on it with a dish towel. We work in companionable silence, and I almost forget that the quiet guy in the hoodie beside me is an explosives expert.

"Thanks for the food," I tell him. "It was really good."

He shrugs. "I like to cook."

"I like to eat."

He shoots me a small smile before falling silent again.

"You didn't have to do that," Grey says, coming in just as we're finishing up.

He carries his own empty plate, and I glance from it to him.

"I know that," I say, "But I clean up my own messes."

"Touché. I'll clean my own mess, then, too."

He heads straight for the sink, and that means he and I will have to stand way too close for comfort, so I slip past him and wander into the next room. Before me, are large windows covered in gauzy curtains and wooden blinds that are open to reveal blooming rose bushes lining the front walkway. Roses in bright crimson reds and soft yellows crowd in amongst greenery and shrubs.

Planters with similar greenery are dotted around the living room, each one strategically placed for access to the best light. The furniture is cozy, the couch made with thick cushions that are more worn than I'd expect for a house made of so much money.

I have the impression someone in Grey's family spends a lot of time here, and it's not Vincenzo. There's too much softness here. Too much peace and quiet.

I'm admiring the tranquil feel of it all when two black SUVs race up the driveway hard enough to kick up gravel in their wake. They grind to a halt and park on either side of Dutch's car, dust clouding up around them.

"Grey," I call, panic rising as I remember how Franco's men drove these exact vehicles.

Grey stalks into the room and looks at the SUVs skidding to a stop outside.

"Crow, get the others," Grey barks.

From the kitchen, the back door opens and closes quickly. My eyes are glued to the cars, though, as the doors open and men in dressy clothes get out. Two wear suits, but the rest are in button-down shirts with the sleeves rolled to the elbows and dark dress pants.

"Who are they?" I ask, throat threatening to close around the words.

"The suits are two of Father's generals," Grey says grimly. He points them out and says, "Ramey's dad and Mia's."

"And the others?"

"Security."

"Oh." I relax as I realize it's not Franco and his men, but Grey senses my relief and turns to me with a dark look.

"They're not here to protect us," he warns.

Before I can ask what he means, two more cars arrive. One is a dark Mercedes, and the other is a bright blue sportscar of some sort that was clearly not made for gravel lanes like this one.

"Shit," Grey mutters.

I look at him, and he explains, "More generals. That one's Razor's old man, and that one's Dutch's."

"So, Mia, Ramsey, Razor, and Dutch are all sons and daughters of a general? What about Crow? Is his dad a general too?" I ask.

"His dad is Razor's dad," Grey says quietly.

"They're brothers."

"Sort of," is all he says.

I want to ask what he means, but then a fifth vehicle pulls in—another SUV. It parks right in front of the porch, blocking everyone else in. My stomach tightens as the driver gets out, looking more like a UFC fighter than a professional chauffeur.

"Get in the kitchen," Grey tells me and then propels me that way by force.

The back door opens as I hurry around the island toward the sink. Mia, Ramsey, Razor, and Dutch all file in. Crow is notably absent, but I don't dare ask where he went as the front door bangs open and men file inside the living room. Mia grabs my arms and pulls me backward a step, tucking me in between her and Razor.

Grey plants himself between the two groups in the open doorway that connects both rooms, his hard gaze on the four generals. They don't say a word to anyone as they spread out in the suddenly-small space. Instead, they all sweep the faces of those present and settle on me.

I swallow hard as I study their faces.

"Razor, you fucking idiot," one of them snarls with a trace of a Hispanic accent. He's taller with dark hair like Razor and has the same broad build and thick arms.

Razor stiffens beside me, but his tone is light as he shrugs and says, "You know me, pops."

The man snorts, his hands fisting at his sides. "You never fucking learn."

"Mia, I swear, you're better than this crowd," says the man Grey pointed out as Mia's father. His hair is a reddish hue though nowhere near as bright her hers.

"That's what I keep telling them, Daddy," she drawls.

The man's eyes flash with irritation.

177

"Ramsey, you and I are going to have that chat I've been promising you," his father says. His golden hair is streaked with gray, but he's toned and even more built than Ramsey is. What is it with these mafia guys and their huge size?

"Bring it, Pops," Ramsey says, the last word dripping with sarcasm.

The man growls, and I tense, wondering if this room is large enough to hold even one of them in wolf form.

Finally, another figure steps in through the front door, and a hush falls over the space. The generals part quickly for him to pass, and he steps to the front. I don't need to see his face to know who it is, but the moment I do, the fury emanating has me shrinking back.

Vincenzo.

The others around me have gone rigid though I don't know if it's from fear, like me, or fury.

"You defied my direct order, you piece of shit," Vincenzo snarls at Grey.

I flinch, but Grey says nothing.

"I should bury you for this," Vincenzo adds.

"Maybe," Grey says evenly. "Though you're the one who begged me to come back to this fucking city. You get what you pay for: isn't that what they say?"

"You fucking ingrate," Vincenzo roars in his face.

Grey blinks but otherwise doesn't react. My heart thunders against my ribcage, fear clogging my throat. Every one of these men looks like they want to kill us. Or at least kill Grey.

And, if even one shifts into a wolf, I'm helpless.

Hell, I'm already helpless against them.

"This is insanity," Vincenzo goes on.

He swings away from Grey to face the rest of us, his angry gaze sweeping from Dutch to Ramsey. "You all violated the sacred respect of a man's home. An attack like that has been against the rules of engagement since this city was created, and in one single morning, you've shit all over our last upheld agreement. Franco's rallying his damned soldiers as we speak. You've just started a fucking war."

"We were already at war the moment you took Lexi," Grey tells him.

I suck in a breath at the way Vincenzo's face reddens as he rounds on his son. "I did not give you permission to speak. And you." He swivels again, marching up to me until he's close enough for me to feel the rage radiating from his body. Mia presses in against me, but it's not reassuring when the monster's sole attention is on me.

"You do not get to make demands. You are not in charge here, do you understand me?"

I bite my tongue against the urge to say something snarky, which would likely get me killed right now. But apparently, his question is not rhetorical. He leans closer so that I flinch back as he roars, "Do you understand me?"

"Yes," I say but Grey walks over and faces his father, nearly wedging himself between us.

Razor and Mia remain where they are, forming a solid wall around me. I swallow hard against the terror choking me, but it remains. Still, I refuse to let him see it, so I keep my chin up and force my breathing to remain even.

"Lexi's agreed to our terms," Grey tells him. "She and I will announce the engagement tonight."

Vincenzo turns to glare at him. "You're damn right you

will. Because, if either one of you has a hair out of place or a single fucking eyelash out of line from here out, I will remind you of your place in this organization. By whatever means necessary."

"Understood," Grey says.

The generals grumble their agreement and irritation. But Vincenzo is practically vibrating with his contained rage.

"Now, you owe me for the blatant disrespect you showed this morning," Vincenzo tells Grey.

"I'm prepared to take the hit," Grey says.

Something about the way he says it sends a chill up my spine. What kind of hit?

"And what about the rest of you?" Vincenzo bellows.

Grey's eyes widen a fraction, but he quickly clamps down on his expression. "No."

"The fuck did you just say?" Vincenzo demands.

"It was all on me," Grey says. "I gave the order. They only followed them."

"Doesn't fucking matter. They all owe for what they did today," Vincenzo says.

"Then I'll pay it all," Grey says, shooting Mia a glare when she tries to argue.

She falls silent again, her hand sliding into mine and squeezing. I keep my surprise at the gesture off my face, and while I don't squeeze back, I don't let go either. My heart thuds as I try to understand what's happening—and what exactly Grey is paying with for his insubordination.

"Fine," Vincenzo says smugly. "Outside. Now." He turns to glance at the rest of us and says, "Stay inside. If a single one of you steps out that door, I'll double his payment."

Everyone bows their head, and I have to bite back a curse at the way he sneers at them, challenging them to argue. But no one does.

Vincenzo shoves past Grey out the back door, and the generals follow.

"Grey," Mia says, but he shakes his head to shush her.

"Don't." He glances from me back to her. "Make sure she stays inside," he adds. "No matter what."

Mia's shoulders sag. "I will."

22

GREY

I stalk through the backyard, not stopping until I'm near the riverbank and hopefully far enough that the view from the kitchen windows is at least partially obstructed. Doesn't matter, though. I already know the squad will feel every single bit of what's to come, which is another reason to get as far from the house as possible. If my father learns we're developing a pack bond again, he won't be satisfied with letting me pay for their sins.

As long as my true family remains out of his reach, I don't care what kind of punishment he gives me.

This is on me, not them.

Near the water's edge, I begin to strip out of my clothes and toss them away. This bullshit isn't worth wasting an outfit. My father, however, doesn't share the same sense of practicality.

He marches toward me, already shifting into his wolf as he comes. His snarl rips from his throat even while he's still human. I shift too, forcing the change as quickly as possible so I can be ready. Not that it'll do me much good, but being ripped into as a wolf is preferable over having my human body shredded by canines and claws.

My father doesn't wait, either.

The minute he reaches me, he growls low and threatening, looming over me until his alpha power cowers my wolf. I grit my teeth against the feeling, hating how out of control I feel when he asserts his dominance this way.

Once, I defied him and resisted it—but that's what landed me in this fucked up mess in the first place. So, if he thinks I'm doing it again now, he's wrong.

For a second, as memories wash over me, I wonder if this is the whole test. Him asserting his dominance if only to see whether I'll fight him a second time. But the moment I lower my head out of deference, he sinks his teeth into my shoulder. Not a test then.

Fuck.

His canines rip straight through muscle, and agony follows.

I make a sound of pain, barely managing to bite back a howl as a chunk of fur and flesh is ripped away.

That's one.

My father's wolf backs away and spits out the mix of blood and fur then snarls at me and comes again. There is absolutely no trace of compassion or remorse in his hateful eyes, nor do I expect there to be. The man is a monster, through and through.

I can feel his enjoyment radiating from his wolf; the satisfaction he gets from taking me apart bite by bite while I'm helpless to fight back. It's sick. And it's exactly why he deserves to be removed from power. So he can never do this to anyone else.

He rips me apart, leaving four more deep gashes in my body. One on each shoulder and two on my left flank for a total of five. He doesn't go for my throat, and I realize, as I sag to the grass, hissing and huffing in pain, that I half-expected him to just end me right here on the riverbank with all my friends watching.

With *her* watching.

With so much of his alpha power flowing at me, I also get glimpses of his thoughts, and I can feel his desire to do just that. But he backs away, his muzzle bloody from the damage he's done to me.

I don't fight back. I couldn't if I wanted to. The weight of his alpha power still hangs over me like a guillotine ready to fall if I resist him. And he wants that too.

A reason to end me. To end the disappointment that I am to him. But then he wouldn't be able to torture me like this anymore.

Finally, he steps back and stares down at me.

I don't bother to look up at him.

If I do, I might just kill him. With his generals standing around, watching the spectacle of a one-sided fight, my odds of surviving a dumb move like that are not good.

Instead, I stay down and wait for him to leave so I can drag myself into the woods and try to heal. But the power around me prickles with an uneasy pressure, and he comes forward again. I tense, confused. Five, that's what I offered to take. One for me and one for each of the general's children—or the heirs they bother to recognize. Unless he's finally decided to acknowledge Crow as a legitimate heir.

The pressure grows stronger until the weight of it presses down around me and shoves my nose into the dirt.

The pressure becomes a buzzing in my ears that seeps into my skin and settles inside my bones. My body tightens and contorts even though I never asked it to. I squeeze my fists and grit my teeth against the pain, but there's no stopping what my father's wolf has ordered of mine.

Slowly, my wolf begins to recede, and I shift back to my human form—against my will, which only makes the process hurt so much fucking worse than it should.

When it's done, I'm face-down, naked, and bleeding from several deep gashes across my body. My father's wolf approaches, towering over me, and I hear his alpha voice in my head.

This one's for the girl.

It takes me a minute to understand what he means. And who. But then I realize he means to take punishment for Lexi too. In his eyes, she's just as much to blame as we are for what happened with Franco, and I volunteered to pay for everyone's mistake. All I can think is that, by forcing my shift, he's decided to leave her alone. Relief makes my shoulders sag heavier than before.

Suddenly, even more than the pain, I feel exhausted.

"Fine," I say. "It's done."

He turns to walk away, and I reach for my wolf, ready to shift back again so that I can begin to heal. These wounds need the power of my wolf form before they become a risk for infection with the way I've just rolled around on the ground. But my wolf remains out of reach.

Panic stirs inside me as I struggle to access it and come up empty.

My father shifts back to human form. I don't bother acknowledging him, but then he leans over me and speaks.

"Your wolf will be inaccessible for a few days. I suggest you get up and dress those wounds properly. You'll need to look the part for tonight's event."

He turns and walks away, and I lift my head enough to watch him go.

One of his security detail walks up and hands him another set of clothes. I watch from my stomach as he disappears into the house along with his entourage of generals.

For a moment, I can only lie here, letting his words sink in and absorbing the shock of what he's done to me. An alpha has complete power and dominance over his pack—including overriding our own access to our beasts. But no alpha has ever used it before. Not like this.

Never, in all of Franco's years as alpha of this city, has he ever suppressed another shifter's wolf.

Neither has my father—until now.

Until me.

The shock doesn't last long, though, because, of course, it would be me he'd inflict this on. I defied him once, and he'll never forget that. He'll never let me stop paying for it either.

Suddenly, my decision to step up earlier is even more important. Because, in this moment, I realize I only ever had two choices anyway. Continue to live under the dominance of my father, or challenge him once and for all. Even if it kills me, I can't live this way forever, which means I never really had a choice at all.

Getting up is harder than I expect. The wounds on my body burn and scream at me as I slowly pull myself to my knees. Without my wolf to help dull the pain and strengthen my body, I feel slow and weak.

I feel human.

From here, the house looks like it's miles away, and I suppress a groan as I push to my feet and start limping toward it. Out front, a car starts, followed quickly by doors opening and closing. I relax a little, knowing the generals are departing.

Hopefully, *he* is too.

A moment later, the rest of the cars start up, and one by one, they all drive away, their tires crunching over gravel. My father's car is the last to go, but when it does, my knees buckle. Exhaustion and pain overwhelm my senses. My chest aches with every single breath.

I grab the low wall near the firepit, disgusted with how slow my progress is and how easily my body is giving out. The back door opens, and a figure comes out. I don't have to look up to know who it is. Even without my wolf, I can feel her.

Lexi doesn't say a word to me as she steps up beside me and slides her arm around my waist. I inhale sharply, but she's careful to keep her hands away from my wounds, and I realize I'm reacting to her soft touch rather than to any pain she's caused me. She doesn't give me a chance to pull away, though. Her other hand grabs my wrist, and she slings my arm over her shoulder, letting me put my weight on her as she slowly walks us toward the house.

Her body against mine is heaven.

This isn't like the lap dance. There's no lust. Well, maybe a little, as evidenced by my dick stirring at the way Lexi's hands press up against my bare skin. But mostly, there's comfort. The feel of Lexi flush against my hip, helping me when I'm at my weakest, stirs a strange feeling in my chest. It's a sensation I haven't felt in years—long before I left this place in search of peace and freedom. And it's so foreign I can't name it. One thing I do know: the cruelty, the pain, the "payment" as he calls it—none of those things strip me bare like Lexi Giovanni with her soft, slender arms holding me upright.

And then I know exactly what this strange feeling is. Having Lexi here beside me feels like home.

23

LEXI

*T*he moment Vincenzo follows Grey out the back door, I press myself against the kitchen window, but Mia pulls me back.

"You don't want to see this," she tells me grimly.

"Yes," I say, pulling out of her grasp. "I do. I have to."

She studies me for a beat and then sighs. "Okay. Come on. You can see better from the bedroom."

She hesitates until all the generals follow Vincenzo out. Then she leads me down the hall and into the first bedroom on the left. It faces the back of the house and, true to her word, offers a large window view of the grassy area where Grey stands.

Vincenzo stalks after him, but it's Grey I stare at, wide-eyed, as he removes his clothing and tosses it aside. First, his shirt, revealing a toned chest and rippled abs, and then his pants, revealing—

Damn.

I swallow hard, my mouth suddenly dry as I take in the sight of him on full display. Tattoos wrap his arms, ending at his shoulder and highlighting how darkly dangerous he can be. A danger that turns me on more than it should. Some part of me is aware of how thirsty I must look, but I can't quite bring myself to care. Grey is breathtaking, and I can't do anything but admire the sight of him so unconcerned with how exposed he is.

If I hadn't been staring like a stalker, I might have missed the first small ripple beneath his skin. But the second and third ones are unmistakable.

My eyes go wide, and now I can't look away for entirely different reasons as his arms and legs begin to stretch and move. Fur sprouts along his skin. His brow furrows in what looks like concentration or intensity. A second later, he falls to his knees, but by the time his hands land, they're giant paws.

Grey is gone, and in his place stands a giant, charcoal-colored wolf. I'd only seen him in this form once, and I'd been so panicked at the time that I'd secretly begun to convince myself I'd imagined the entire thing.

But there's no imagining this.

And to make it more surreal, I watch as Vincenzo shifts too. He doesn't bother removing his clothes first and instead just shreds them as he shifts mid-stride. His wolf is so dark brown he's nearly black, and his lips are already pulled back in an angry snarl. He stalks over to where Grey stands and leans over him until Grey's wolf lowers his head.

"What's happening?" I ask Mia.

She stands a couple of feet away, also watching the two wolves. Her forehead is creased with some internal effort.

She doesn't look away from them as she tells me, "Vincenzo is using his alpha power to make Grey submit."

"Why?" I ask.

"So he can't fight back."

Her words are punctuated by a snarl loud enough to hear through the window. I swing my gaze back to the two wolves just in time to see Vincenzo ripping a chunk out of Grey's shoulder. Blood leaks from the open wound, and I gasp.

"We have to help him." I dart out of the room and am halfway down the hall when Ramsey appears, blocking my way. His expression is pinched.

"Move," I say, "Vincenzo's hurting him."

"I know," he says quietly, but he doesn't move.

"We have to help," I say, trying to shove him, but the guy's like a brick wall.

"We can't go out there," Ramsey says sadly.

I stare at him as another yelp sounds from outside. My heart squeezes as I think of Grey being hurt because of what we did. No, because of what I asked him to do.

"What is wrong with you?" I demand, my panic building to a breaking point. "We can't just let him be attacked by his own father."

"He chose it," Mia says tightly.

"What difference does that make if he's hurting?" I demand.

"He's not the only one," Ramsey says, wincing as a third yelp sounds.

The sound of it nearly breaks me. All I can think is how this is all my fault. His pain is on my shoulders. It makes me desperate to do something. Anything but stand here and watch helplessly.

I turn and shove her aside, racing back to the bedroom in time to see Vincenzo biting Grey's flank and ripping a wound wide open. My breath catches. It's horrific—the blood and flesh being exposed is awful, but the fact that all four generals are standing and watching in calm silence is beyond anything I've ever witnessed before. Not to mention the ones here in the house with me.

Grey's *friends*.

Mia and Ramsey hover in the doorway behind me, probably to make sure I don't leave this room again.

Ugh.

"What kind of friends leave their leader to suffer like this alone?" I demand, feeling vicious in my helplessness.

Mia doesn't react, but Ramsey's eyes flash with guilt before he looks away from me.

Fucking cowards.

I turn back to the window as Vincenzo steps back, his wolf still hovering near where Grey has fallen on his belly. Then, slowly, Grey's body begins to shift like before. Except, this is nothing like last time. It's a slow-motion version with limbs cracking and moving in ways that don't look natural compared to his earlier shift. Whatever's happening has the two behind me sucking in a breath and making grunting sounds of frustration and pain.

"What's going on?" I demand.

"He's forcing him to shift," Ramsey says, his voice strained.

"Can he do that?" I ask.

"As alpha of the Diavolo pack, yeah, technically, he can," Mia whispers.

I look at them, noting the way Mia's face has gone white.

"What's wrong?" I ask.

"We formed a pack bond with Grey, which means we feel some of what he feels right now," Ramsey tells me.

I study them, noting the way Mia's biting her lip now and Ramsey's hands are fisted at his sides. My heart thuds heavily, both with panic and concern. I'm still figuring out how all this pack hierarchy works, but that's the least of my concerns right now.

Finally, I turn back to the window and watch as Grey's body slowly becomes human again. He lies unmoving on his stomach as Vincenzo turns and walks away from him. The generals stay put until Vincenzo passes them, shifting back to his human form as he approaches the house. Someone passes the alpha a set of clothes, which he snags as he heads for the back door. I brace myself for him to come in here, my fear and fury merging until I'm not sure if I want him to come for me next or just leave without a word.

In the end, it's not up to me anyway.

Mia and Ramsey step inside the bedroom, and Ramsey closes the door with a soft click, shutting us in together. No one speaks as we listen to Vincenzo move through the house, getting dressed and calling orders to his men. The other generals file back into the house, and a moment later, the front door opens as they all exit to the parking area.

Judging from the sound of their voices, Vincenzo is the last to leave, but when the door shuts behind him, I breathe a sigh of relief. Glancing out the window, I see that Grey has managed to get to his feet. He's bleeding and dirty and walking like he might keel over at any moment.

Determined, I step up to where Ramsey blocks the door. "Let me out."

I half-expect him to fight me but, instead, he flicks a glance at Mia, who apparently gives him whatever answer he needs.

He moves silently aside.

I fling open the door and hurry down the hall and outside. Grey falters as he reaches the patio, but I'm already there, grabbing him and helping him make it the rest of the way.

His skin is warm, and while I'm careful not to touch his wounds, he tenses when I wrap my hand around his ribs. Grabbing his other wrist, I drape his tattooed arm over my shoulder so he can lean on me for support. The worst part is that he lets me, and I know that speaks to how injured and weak he is in this moment. The Grey I'm used to would never show this kind of vulnerability.

My heart aches for him. Despite everything he's done, he didn't deserve this. I'm aware that he's still naked, but it's not the distraction it was before, not when he's struggling to even remain upright. Not when he's bloody and beaten—because of me.

Dutch appears at the back door, holding it open for us to pass inside. As we do, he holds a towel out that I help Grey wrap around his waist.

"What the fuck," Dutch says to him. "Why don't you shift back and heal? Old man's gone. Coast is clear."

"I can't," Grey says flatly.

We make it to the kitchen as the others appear. Ramsey, Razor, Mia—even Crow is suddenly back. They all stare at Grey, dumbfounded by his answer.

"What do you mean you can't?" Razor demands.

"I mean my wolf isn't available," Grey says.

"He blocked your wolf, didn't he?" Mia asks.

Grey grunts, and they all stare at him with varying masks of horror and rage.

"I don't understand," I say. "How is it possible that someone else can keep you from shifting?"

"An alpha is the only one of us who has the power to take away that ability," Crow says quietly when no one else speaks up.

"None of them has actually fucking done it," Dutch growls.

"Not even Franco's that evil," Ramsey says.

"No one's that evil," Grey replies.

"Vincenzo's a son of a bitch," Razor says, punching his palm with his fist. "He deserves—"

"We're still standing in his house," Mia points out, cutting him off with a pointed look.

Razor mumbles but doesn't argue. I glance around, worried Vincenzo is somehow still listening, but there's no sign of cameras. Clearly, they're paranoid for a reason though.

"If he can't shift, he can't heal," Ramsey says grimly.

No one says anything to that.

I bite my tongue, not wanting to distract further with my questions. "He needs a hospital," I say instead.

That gets them on the same page instantly.

"Hell no," Grey growls at the same time they all echo his sentiment.

"We can't," Mia says more gently than the others.

"Do you see his wounds?" I demand. "He needs stitches."

"Hospitals will ask questions," she tells me.

"And? Aren't all the doctors in your pocket or something?"

"Not all of them," she says, "And that doesn't help us anyway. They'll see Vincenzo's attack on Grey a clear casting of blame for the mess at Franco's earlier. They'll see it as disloyalty and conflict within the family. Best case, it sends more votes Franco's way. Worst case, it turns them against Grey entirely, and they try to put him down for what they perceive as a crime against both Vincenzo and Franco."

"They'll see him as a traitor," Dutch adds grimly.

"Vincenzo deserves to be charged for this," I say, refusing to back down. How can they just stand here and let it go?

"He wouldn't be," Mia says sadly.

Maybe it's the worry coming through her words rather than raw fury like the others, but I believe her that taking Grey to a hospital will only make things worse politically. Doesn't mean he's out of the woods physically though.

"Fine then. Do you at least have a First Aid kit?"

"Last bedroom on the left," Grey says. "Master bathroom."

"Come on."

With my support, we head that way. None of the others follow, and I don't know if it's their rage needing a cooling-off period or if they simply trust me to handle this. Several times, I've been the one to patch kids up at the shelter when they've gotten hurt living on the street, but I don't have any experience patching up wounds quite this bad.

With my arm still around Grey's waist, I lead us back into a large bedroom with enough white and neutral tones that I wince at the stains left by his dirty, blood-streaked footprints.

He doesn't even seem to notice them.

In the bathroom, Grey perches on the wide edge of a jacuzzi tub ringed in marble. His handprint leaves smudges of blood that have my throat closing in guilt and worry. The ink on his arms is smudged with dirt and blood, obscuring most of the design, but up close I can finally see that's a beautifully intricate pattern of lines and symbols. For a moment, I blink at him, forgetting what we came in here for.

His voice brings me back.

"Down there."

He points at the cabinet beneath the sink, and I rummage through until I find the First Aid kit. The longer it takes, the more frantic I become. Fumbling for bandages and ointment, I nearly drop them all, thanks to my trembling fingers.

"Lexi." Grey's voice, though gentle, is sharp enough to make me still as I look up. "It's okay. I'm okay."

For some reason, his reassurance pisses me off.

"You're *not* okay," I say hotly as I go back to ripping the bandages open harder than necessary. "What your father just did to you is barbaric."

"Well then, it fits since that's what we are."

"You're wolves. That doesn't mean you have to be inhumane."

He looks up at me, his expression twisting sardonically. "To be humane, you'd have to be an actual human first."

"Are you really arguing semantics while you bleed out into your father's bathtub?"

He glances over to see his blood trailing into the white porcelain. "This is my tub," he says, which is the least of any problems I've pointed out.

I roll my eyes and step closer, ready with the alcohol and gauze. He looks at me, and I don't bother trying to sugarcoat anything.

"This is going to hurt," I tell him quietly.

"I'm already hurt," he mutters.

The moment I press the alcohol-soaked pad against his skin, his whole body jerks. "Fuck," he says loudly.

"I told you," I mutter.

He goes silent, and I look up to see him giving me a wry look. "Your bedside manner is a little rough around the edges, nurse."

"Maybe it's because my patient is a stubborn wiseass."

His lips twitch. "Maybe."

I move to the next gash along his shoulder and pause there. "Ready?"

"Do it."

He lets loose another sharp hiss but without the cursing. I do it twice more, relieved to see the gashes aren't bleeding as much as they were before.

"Maybe your wolf healing is helping you after all," I say.

He looks down at the gash on his leg with a frown. "I've

been trying to force it to come back to me since that asshole left, but I think this is as good as it'll get."

"I can bandage these with gauze, but that's as good as I can get, too," I tell him as I start bandaging and taping everything up.

When I'm done, I toss all the trash and stand. Grey stands too, and the towel he had draped over his lap falls to the floor. Now that he's not bleeding out, I can't help but notice the perfectly shaped V that points like an arrow to his very impressive cock.

He doesn't move to cover himself either. Instead, he simply waits, watching me as I drink him in.

My breath catches.

This isn't about bandages anymore.

This is Grey wanting me to see him.

Dragging my gaze back to his, I note the heavy-lidded stare he gives me, and my core tightens with how much I want to feel him touch me.

"You like what you see, princess?" he asks.

My heart hammers in my chest, and I have to force the words from my suddenly dry mouth. "Yes."

"Come here."

He reaches for me, grabbing my arm and pulling me against his bare chest before I can argue. Not that I will. If I'm being honest, which I've spent days trying *not* to be, I've wanted this since the moment I found him waiting for me in the VIP room at Shady's.

From the moment I agreed to that lap dance and lowered my body over his on that couch, I've been waiting to finish this. The way our bodies fit together feels like some missing piece has been found. The way he touches me now only makes my wanting him more agonizing than ever.

In this moment, he's not my enemy. Or, if he is, I no longer care. Not so long as he puts his hands on me and finishes what we started in that back room.

The moment my chest is flush against his, he releases my arm only to snake his hand around my waist and press me even closer. My nipples drag against him, hardened to peaks from the way he studies my reaction to him. Even the friction of my shirt between us turns me on.

"You're beautiful when you fight me," he says. "But you're irresistible after you've finally given in."

His mouth closes over mine with complete possession.

At his words, I want to fight him some more, but he's right. I've given in to him already, and there's no going back now. I melt against him, opening myself fully when we've barely just begun.

His free hand cups the back of my neck, angling my mouth so he can devour me completely. I cling to him, my knees already threatening to buckle with the sensation of him. But he shows absolutely no mercy, shoving his tongue inside my mouth like he has every right to claim me this way.

He kisses me like he kidnaps—taking and taking as if he's owed everything simply by wanting it in the first place. I should hate it, but I've never craved more of something like I crave Grey.

My hand brushes the gauze on his shoulder, and he winces against my mouth.

"Sorry," I say quickly, pulling it away.

"Don't be sorry," he says sharply.

I look up at him, startled to see the fire in his gaze. There's more than desire behind that heat, and it terrifies me just as much as it thrills me to see it there.

"I just meant that you're hurting. Because of me," I tell him.

But he shakes his head, and his eyes glint like the tip of a knife. "None of this is your fault, Lexi. Don't apologize for it. Ever. My father did this. And your grandfather too. And I'm going to make them all pay."

"We," I correct. "We will make them all pay. Together."

"We," he agrees, stroking my hair. "I fucking swear it."

LEXI

The night sky offers a beautiful backdrop for the rooftop gathering. My dress, one of the gowns Grey picked out for me, is a navy blue with sequins that reflect the twinkle lights strung around the pergola. So much so that the rich fabric shimmers blindingly with every movement of my body. I frown, trying to hold still so the damn thing will stop feeling so freaking extra.

I've never been this dressed up in my life, and it feels strange to do it now for all these people who think they know me but have no idea. In fact, I might have chosen something else entirely if Grey's eyes hadn't nearly fallen out of his head when I walked out of my bedroom earlier. Having him look at me like that made me feel powerful, but now that I'm here, it's not just his reaction that matters. If I'm not perfect, Vincenzo will take it out on his son, and I refuse to be the cause of that kind of violence again.

Grey's injuries are painful; I can see it in the stiff way he carries himself. He looks achingly handsome in his tux, and the way he stands with his arm around my waist, constantly reminding me I'm not alone, is a distraction from the guilt.

Now, I stand on the rooftop of one of the city's fanciest restaurants, a place called Chavez—and everyone here eyes me like I'm a specimen in a petri dish. We've been here all of thirty minutes, and already I'm buckling under their scrutiny.

Guests stare openly, but it's the generals and, more specifically, their wives, who don't bother keeping their voices down when I come to stand beside where they're all hovering around a waist-high cocktail table. Each of them clutches a martini in their jewel-laden hands, their noses turned stiffly toward the sky while they judge everyone else.

One of them shoots me a glance and remarks, "Her tits are completely unrealistic. She should have gone with a smaller size to make it believable."

I roll my eyes but don't bother to give them my attention. They aren't worth it.

Another responds, "I think she's actually really pretty for a stripper."

I move away so I can't hear them just in case my patience snaps and I decide to break one of their very expensive noses.

Across the crowded rooftop, Grey nods at whatever his father is saying to him. The older man's shoulders are squared, and Grey's expression is tight, but otherwise, they remain civil enough in front of the guests. Still, I'm not interested in speaking to the elder Diavolo, no matter how good his manners are tonight.

Scanning the other guests, I shift a little, and my dress

twinkles brightly with the slight movement. The gown Grey insisted on is beautiful and ostentatious to the point of discomfort.

Just then, Mia walks up. "Are you okay?"

"Fine, why?"

She arches a brow, clearly not buying my answer. "You look like you ate something terrible."

"It's not the food," I tell her.

"Then what—?"

"This dress."

"It's gorgeous."

"I look like a disco ball," I tell her, gesturing to my dress. "I'm going to walk across the room, and someone's going to have a stroke."

Mia laughs. "So dramatic."

I raise my brows at that. "You guys will literally kill someone over a girl you've never met, and you think I'm dramatic?"

"Fair," she admits with a pout. "But it's not just about you. I mean, look around. What do you see?"

"Champagne. Expensive clothes I could never afford. A level of self-involvement I couldn't reach if I tried."

"Don't forget self-importance," she adds wryly.

"You say that like it's a bad thing," Ramsey says, joining us on my other side with a drink in his hand. "What's wrong with being important?"

I glance over, appreciating the way he fills out a suit. They're all gorgeous, in fact. Mia with her black gown that hangs from her shoulders from one slanted strap, her throat and ears dripping in diamonds. Dutch standing not far away with his shirt sleeves rolled to the forearms, revealing the tattoos wrapping around his arms like snakes. Razor and Crow sit at a table in the back with heads bent close. They've already shucked their jackets and bow ties, leaving the top few buttons of their shirts open to reveal smooth skin and sharply angled chests beneath.

The general's children are beautiful, every single one.

Beautiful and deadly.

But it's Grey who takes my breath away.

"Lexi's worried she'll hurt someone in that dress," Mia tells him.

Ramsey scoffs. "She's going to break every heart in this room the moment they realize she's taken."

He winks.

Mia snickers, eyes narrowing even as she manages to keep her demure smile in place. "Most of the assholes in this room deserve to be hurt anyway."

While the two of them continue to banter, I scan the guests until my gaze lands on Grey. He's near the bar, talking to a woman I don't know. She's elegant in a navy-blue gown that hugs her slender frame and understated jewelry that lets her mature beauty shine.

Jealousy streaks through me. Not only at the sight of him talking to another woman but at the idea that he has this whole life here with family and friends he's known forever, and I have … nothing.

No history, no roots. No future.

"You can stop shooting daggers, you know." Mia's voice snaps me out of my intense study, and I look over at her. "That's his mother."

"I wasn't—"

"Uh-huh."

The longer I look back and forth between them, the more I begin to note the way Grey's brows slant just like hers do. The shape of their mouths is similar too, especially when they frown—which they both do now as if whatever Grey has just said to her was unhappy news.

My cheeks flush, and I duck my head, deciding now is as good a time as any to down the rest of the drink I've been nursing. Mia, gratefully, doesn't comment further, and a moment later, the band finishes their song.

Vincenzo makes his way forward and steps onto the low stage before grabbing a mic. My stomach clenches, both in fury at the sight of him and in fear at what's to come.

"Here," Mia mutters and takes my empty champagne flute, replacing it with a full one. Our eyes meet, and she nods at me in understanding. "One more won't hurt."

I take her advice and drain the bubbly. The buzz it offers isn't much, but it dulls my nerves at least a little.

Up front, Vincenzo calls for attention, and I take a deep breath then exhale it shakily.

Here we go.

"Good evening, and thank you all for coming," Vincenzo says with a smile I know only masks the evil beneath.

Grey breaks away from the woman—his mother—and makes his way toward me. Ramsey steps aside to give him room, and Grey presses in close and slides his arm around my waist. The pressure of his warm fingers at my hip is a reassurance I desperately need.

"Just breathe," he whispers.

I glance up at him and find support in his dark gaze.

Suddenly, for the first time since he brought me to Indigo Hills, it's like we're in this together.

Allies.

Maybe more…

"It's an honor to be among friends as tonight is a special evening for my family—and our pack," Vincenzo says, and I face the front again. "I can't think of anyone I'd want to share this moment with than all of you. I'd like to officially announce that my son, Jericho Diavolo, has chosen Lexi Giovanni as his mate and future bride."

The crowd applauds as every single one of them turns to look at us. No, not us. *Me.* And while there are mostly polite smiles being tossed my way, there is also a distinct feeling of judgment from the guests nearby.

"Congratulations to the lovely couple," Vincenzo says. "Come on up here, you crazy kids."

"Your name is Jericho?" I whisper.

"Only to him." His hand finds mine. "Come on."

Mia snags my empty flute out of my hand just as Grey tugs me up to the stage. Every single pair of eyes is glued to my back, but I keep my shoulders square and chin up, refusing to let them see me sweat.

Years of locking away my emotions from others make their scrutiny slightly easier. Still, I squeeze Grey's hand tightly as we come to stand beside Vincenzo. I don't miss the way Grey puts himself between me and his father—or the stiffness with which he stands beside the man who nearly killed him hours earlier.

I squeeze his hand once more for that.

"Son, why don't you say a few words," Vincenzo urges.

Grey takes the mic, and Vincenzo beams at him expectantly.

"Thank you all for coming," Grey says in a voice that is coldly charming. It's not one I've ever heard him use before, and I can't help but watch him as he plays the part Vincenzo has demanded even better than I realized he knew how. "I know what most of you are thinking. What is an amazing catch like Lexi doing with a nobody like me?"

A few laughs, all of them strained.

"But seriously," he says, expression intent now as he looks out at the faces. "Lexi and I are aware of the tension that exists between our families. We know this union is a shock for many of you. We won't pretend our decision doesn't affect the entire pack. Hell, the entire city. But this city and our families are what brought us together, and through getting to know Lexi, I've come to learn she's as devoted to helping as I am. I know we can make a bigger difference together than apart. I hope we can even forge peace for the first time in our history. Lexi and I are committed to this city and to one another. We ask for your support and faith as we move forward."

"Does this mean you're home for good?" someone calls out, and I swear the voice sounds a lot like Dutch though I can't see who spoke.

"I am," Grey confirms. "It's time to take my rightful place among my pack."

The crowd's applause is much louder than before and much more genuine if the expressions are any indication. The faith Grey has asked them for is already being offered here and now—only, it's Grey they're looking at, not me.

And not Vincenzo.

Grey hands his father the microphone, but Vincenzo frowns and stalks over to me, holding the mic out.

"Your turn," he says in a low, menacing tone.

I grip the microphone tightly to hide the tremble. Blinking out at the crowd, my nerves cloud my vision until I can't see faces—only blurred figures. My heart slams against my chest, and I have to shove the images of Grey's torn body from my mind so I can shove out the words Vincenzo wants to hear.

"I'd like to echo everything my fiancé said and to say thank you for the warm welcome you've shown me tonight. I look forward to being a part of the Diavolo family."

The applause when I'm done is a soft roar in my ears thanks to my heart pounding loudly enough to drown it out.

Vincenzo isn't satisfied yet, though. He lowers the mic, covering it with his hand so his voice can't carry as he glares at us both. "Now seal it."

I look back at him, confused, but then Grey grabs my elbow and turns me to face him, and I know exactly what he means to do. Grey steps in close, his gaze warm and reassuring as he braces his palm along my jaw.

"Pretend it's just us," he whispers.

Then he leans in and brushes my lips with his own.

The crowd is delighted. More applause, more smiles and whistles.

Grey's lips curve against mine, and I find myself smiling along with him. My stomach dances with butterflies as he brushes my mouth with his. The engagement we announced might be fake, but what I feel when Grey kisses me is all too real.

Vincenzo snags the mic from my hand. "Clearly, they're smitten," he says with that fake charm dripping once again.

I tense, but Grey doesn't seem done with me yet. He places another soft kiss at the edge of my mouth and another on my cheek. Finally, one more along my jaw. I relax, even knowing we're still on full display for the crowd. Some part of me knows he's only playing the part, convincing them this is real. But, in this moment, it is real. At least, for me.

I sigh against him, and he whispers, "Let's get out of here."

He pulls away, and I nod at him in relief. Hand in hand, he leads me back through the crowd. Many guests call out to him as we pass, offering warm wishes and congratulations. He smiles, nods, and keeps us moving toward the back where the exit to the elevators waits, and I'm so grateful to be done with this whole performance.

In the foyer, the woman from earlier waits.

She smiles at me. "Hello, Lexi. I'm Serena Diavolo, Jericho's mother."

"Hello," I say, taking her hand in mine. "It's a pleasure to meet you."

"Likewise."

I glance at Grey. "Jericho?"

"Don't start," he warns.

His mother looks between us, amused.

"You've been using an alias?" I ask.

"My middle name is Grey," he explains.

"Jericho Grey Diavolo," I say, and he scowls.

His mother chuckles. "He only ever heard that when there was hell to pay."

"I'll remember that," I say, shooting him a smug look.

She laughs, eyes twinkling at Grey. "I like her."

The compliment warms me, and when she looks back at me, her smile is soft but genuine. "You both did well up there."

Where Vincenzo is all violence and forced power, Serena is softness and sweet. There's a look in her eyes, a sort of sadness that suggests she knows exactly what was at stake tonight. I wonder if she's been at the wrong end of her husband's wrath just like Grey has.

She glances at Grey, adding, "He's happy with it."

Grey shakes his head. "Happy is not a word that could ever describe him."

"You know what I mean."

He sighs. "I do. Listen, I'm taking Lexi home. I know it's going to piss him off, but—"

"I'll take care of it," she says, shooing us along.

But Grey hesitates. "You sure you're up for it? You promised to take some time away."

Serena smiles and glances at me. "I couldn't miss the announcement of my son's engagement, could I?"

"Mom," Grey begins, but she shakes her head, cutting him off.

"Go," she urges. "Enjoy yourselves. Don't be a stranger, Lexi. Let's do brunch very soon."

"I'd like that," I tell her, offering a genuine smile.

"I'd like it too," she tells me as she hits the call button and the elevator doors open. "Now, go," she says firmly.

Grey kisses her cheek as we pass. "Thanks, Mom. Love you."

"Love you too, darling. Good night."

We wave as the doors close behind us.

When we're alone, I exhale in relief.

"Your mom seems—"

My words are cut short as Grey grabs me and backs me into the corner of the elevator. My breath catches, and for a moment, I'm too surprised to react. His gaze has darkened, and his hands roam my hips as he presses himself into me.

"I'm sorry," he says, his kind words at war with the intensity of his presence. "For putting you through that."

"Don't be sorry," I whisper. "Don't ever be sorry for me."

His eyes flash as he realizes I'm quoting his words back to him.

"You did a good job tonight, princess."

"I had you beside me," I whisper.

His growl is the last thing I hear before he kisses me like he's not sorry for a fucking thing. And neither am I.

25

GREY

*F*rom the moment I laid eyes on Lexi earlier tonight, she has consumed me. I thought she'd been in my head before, but that lap dance was only the beginning. Back then, I wanted her body, and now I want every single piece of her she'll let me have. Every thought, every breath, every urge has been for this. She's soft and pliant in my arms, already open and willing to give me whatever I want to take. But I refuse to fully take her in this elevator. Not that I have a single qualm about claiming her wherever I please, but it won't be nearly enough time for what I want to do to her. I need more. I need all of her. Not to mention the fact that my injured body probably can't handle this particular position of exertion.

When the elevator dings on the ground floor, I reluctantly step back, straightening her dress before holding the door open for her to exit. The disappointment reflected in her glassy gaze is enough to make my dick twitch, but I merely grin at her—a promise of what's to come—and tug her out into the night with me.

"Come on," I tell her, "Let's get you home and out of these clothes."

"Yes, please," she says, breathless.

Our driver waits, parked at the curb just like I instructed him to be when we arrived. Not that I'd planned on taking her to bed, exactly, but I know from experience with my father's parties that Lexi wouldn't want to stay beyond the point of fulfilling our duty. I climb in behind her, getting a face full of ass before she sits on the far side to make room for me. It takes all my control not to shove her face-first into the backseat and pull her dress up so I can bury my face in her right here.

The image of it causes a hungry growl to slip free from my throat. But it's the look Lexi gives me in response that makes it impossible not to touch her. As the driver comes around, I grab her around the neck and pull her in, claiming her mouth once more. She tastes deliciously sweet—a flavor that's already an addiction and a weakness I plan to give in to again and again.

My hands explore, roaming the fabric of her dress and delving beneath it to skim over the curve of her breasts.

Still, my desire for her rages, and I know it's more than just human lust I feel. My wolf wants her too, even if he can't say so at this moment. He's wanted her since the moment he laid eyes on her in that club. And tonight, I'm done questioning or resisting it.

Pulling my jacket off, I drape it over her legs. Lips swollen from my kiss, she looks at me questioningly but doesn't argue. Moving my hand beneath the fabric, I find the slit in her dress and slip my hand between her legs. My fingertips run along her smooth, silky thighs, and she shivers.

I lean in close to her ear and whisper, "Have I told you how beautiful you look tonight, princess?"

"You—Oh."

She bites her lip as my fingers slip beneath the flimsy fabric of her panties and find her folds, teasing her and running over her clit until she squirms in her seat.

Yes. Squirm for me. Move for me. Come for me.

"Have I told you that you look stunning?" I go on, enjoying the way my compliments seem to make her more desperate for me.

"You haven't," she whispers, breathless as she grips my shirt like it's a life raft.

Rather than rescue her, I slide a finger inside her, and she gasps. Her wetness makes my cock harden instantly.

"Sshh," I tell her.

I can't help but grin at the way she glares at me. Slowly, I slide my finger out of her and tease her wetness again, but she whimpers at the loss, rocking her hips to meet me all while her shimmering gaze silently pleads for more.

"You were exactly what I needed you to be tonight," I tell her quietly. "Perfectly poised. Charming. Gorgeous. Lovely." With every word, I pump my finger in and out of her hot, wet pussy. Then, I drop my voice as I add, "Sexy. Delicious. Dessert."

"Grey," she says, a whispered plea.

I grin, sliding out long enough to add another finger. "Yes?"

"Yes," she confirms, already half-moaning.

I swallow her sounds with a kiss, pumping in and out of

her beneath the jacket still draped across her lap. She moves against me, meeting me, and I can feel her walls squeezing around me as her pleasure builds.

The driver turns the radio up, but I can't bring myself to give two shits that he knows what's going on. All that matters or exists in this moment is her. Pleasing her. Touching her. Having her come apart for me—finally.

Kissing a trail along her jaw to her ear, I whisper, "I'm going to fuck you just like this when we get home. Except I'll have you naked by then. And I'll bury my cock inside you until you scream."

She squeezes around me, her lips parting, and my cock twitches at the thought of being inside her as she closes around me. As she comes.

Almost home, I tell myself, finally noticing the city outside the window as we speed along its streets.

"Almost there, princess," I whisper, knowing full well she's not lasting the drive.

When she comes for me, I swallow her sounds with a kiss.

26

LEXI

My orgasm sends me soaring, and by the time I've finally managed to bring myself down to Earth again, the car is slowing in front of Grey's building, and the driver is coming around to open my door. I look at Grey, who still watches me with a devious sort of delight—clearly enjoying the way he's sent me reeling with his magic fingers—but he only grins and waits for me to collect myself.

"You're evil," I say.

He laughs. "You have no idea."

Glaring at him, I turn away and climb out of the car. Grey steps out behind me and says something to the driver. I concentrate on calming my racing heart, enjoying the cool night air on my flushed skin. Every nerve ending sings from the way he's just made me feel, but it's not enough. I need more. I need Grey like I need oxygen, and until I have him, nothing else matters.

"This way, princess." He tugs my hand toward the glass

doors gilded in gold that mark the main entrance of his apartment building.

"Oh, I get to use the front door this time?" I toss back at him.

He winks. "Unless you prefer the back door."

My face heats at what he's insinuated. "Jericho Grey Diavolo, where are your manners?"

He stops me just outside the doors, expression darkening as he leans in close. "No one calls me that."

"Actually, your mom said it's reserved for when you're in trouble. And I'd say you are."

He glares at me with a glint in his stormy eyes that steals my breath. "Princess, the only one in trouble here is you. Now, let's go before I take you right here on the street."

I shudder because damn if I don't want whatever punishment he's offering to give me. His watchful eye doesn't miss my reaction either.

"That's what I thought." Flashing a devilish grin, he leads me through the lobby doors, which is a new view of the luxury apartments considering I've only ever entered from his private elevator inside the parking garage. The lobby floor gleams white beneath a chandelier that hangs high overhead. Two uniformed guards nod at us from behind the tall desk.

"Evening, Mr. Diavolo," one of them calls.

Grey dips his chin and keeps me moving. His hand on my back is firm and possessive. Like he's done being careful or keeping his distance. I'm not sure when we both decided to stop pretending we don't want each other, but now that I've given in to him, I'm impatient for more.

We can't get upstairs fast enough.

Inside the elevator, he turns to me, and I brace myself for more of the roughness he used when we left the party. But this time, when he kisses me, it's slow and deep. Like a long drink of water from a thirsty man. Somehow, I feel more claimed in this kiss than I ever have.

And I offer him all of me, without a single shred of hesitation.

Somewhere in the back of my mind, I know this can't last. The truce we're calling in order to come together like this is way too fragile, considering the uncertainty of the future. I tell myself I can keep this from becoming too personal even while that voice inside my head screams at me for the lie.

The elevator opens to his apartment, but for a moment, he stands here, kissing me lazily. His hand is snug against the back of my neck, angling me just right so his tongue can taste me at his pace.

It should have been more than enough considering he's already given me one mind-blowing orgasm, but already I can feel my own desire building into something more demanding.

"Grey," I say, breathless and already coming out of the front of my dress thanks to his roaming hand. "I need more."

He flashes a devilish smile. "Oh, there's plenty more in store for you, princess. I'm only just getting started."

He leads me back to his bedroom, and suddenly that line between lust and intimacy blurs even further.

I hesitate, but he tugs me harder.

"What is it?" he asks, pulling me flush against him.

"This is your room. It feels…personal."

"It *is* personal," he agrees, trailing kisses down my throat. When he meets the fabric of my dress, he moves it away to continue kissing my neck and my chest. His mouth finds my breast, and I tip my head back to give him better access, sighing with pleasure.

He straightens, yanking me back to reality when his mouth leaves my skin. I open my eyes to find him watching me intently.

"Tell me you want this," he says.

"What?"

"I need to hear you say the words, Lexi. I need to know you're not going to use this against me later. You're not my prisoner, do you understand me?"

"I want this," I say, my heart fluttering as the words reach my ears.

They're true.

More than that, they're new territory for us.

Suddenly, I don't know the rules anymore.

His eyes darken, and he leans in again, his mouth skimming my jaw with feathery light kisses. My fear eases. This is Grey. He is a lot of things, but he won't hurt me. Not like this.

"I want this," I say again. "I want you."

"I've wanted you since the moment I first saw you," he tells me.

His kisses become sharp nips with his teeth. I cling to him, pleasure and need building in my core. His hands reach for the strap of my dress, and I feel a slight tug against the fabric. Then, it snaps, and the whole thing falls off my body, pooling at my feet.

"Since that moment, I've wanted to see all of you," he murmurs, stepping back and scanning the length of me with dark, hungry eyes that leave my skin tingling in their wake. "I've wanted to touch all of you."

"Do it," I tell him, brave at the way he drinks me in, clearly enjoying what he sees.

"Take off your bra."

I obey him immediately.

My heart thunders against my ribs as I reach back and unclasp the strapless bra then let it fall at my feet.

"Now your panties."

I slide out of them too, aware that I'm fully submitting to his orders now. To his dominance—a dominance that only turns me on even more.

Standing naked before him leaves me vulnerable and exposed, but his declarations about wanting me make me braver.

"I want to see you," I tell him, stepping closer and reaching for his bow tie. It comes undone in my fingers, and I toss it aside then start on his shirt buttons. He stands, letting me undress him as he grazes my skin with his fingers. I peel off his shirt and unbutton his pants, one by one, removing items until he's completely naked before me. His bandages have held, and I'm glad because I don't want to stop to play nurse—not yet.

I lick my lips, unable to keep from staring at the hard lines of his chest, the rippled abs, and the deep V that leads to his cock already sprung to attention.

My hand closes over it, and he hisses.

Then, it's as if the spell is broken. He kisses me hungrily, his tongue plunging inside my mouth, demanding even before I can offer myself up. My hand slides up and down the length of him, and he snarls from deep in his throat.

His arms come around my waist, and he lifts me, depositing me on the bed with a grunt. I want to ask if he's all right, but something about the way he watches me keeps me from questioning him. He lowers himself to me, his hand cupping my breast as he takes a nipple into his mouth.

"Yes." I exhale, arching into the heat of his mouth and the delicious flick of his tongue. "More."

"Mmm." He releases that nipple only to do the same to the other. "How much more?"

I rock my hips, need quickly bordering on desperation. Whatever satisfaction that first orgasm offered is gone. My body craves him, and my mind is lost to everything else.

"All of it," I tell him.

His fingers dip inside me, driving so hard inside me that my breath catches.

"So wet and ready for me," he murmurs, staring down at me as he fucks me with two fingers. "Good girl."

He draws away and positions himself at my entrance. The tip of his cock brushes my clit, and I arch upward to meet him.

"Good girl," he whispers again.

He slides inside me in one quick stroke, and I gasp as he fills and stretches me so perfectly. When he begins to move, the pleasure overtakes my senses, and I'm lost to everything except him. The way he makes me feel is beyond anything I've ever experienced.

"Open your eyes," he commands, and I do, unaware I'd even closed them. "Stay with me, princess."

"I'm right here," I pant.

My hips rock, meeting him stroke for stroke.

His eyes never leave mine, his gaze intent as he propels me higher and higher toward my release. I wrap my arms around his shoulders, careful to keep away from his bandages but determined to feel as much of his skin as I can. He increases the pace, rocking me hard enough to send the headboard against the wall.

"Grey," I say, panting hard as my walls begin to clench around him.

"Let me see you come," he says, his voice rough. "Now."

The command is all I need to do exactly as he says. Behind my eyelids, stars explode as I soar with the force of my orgasm. Grey gasps, tensing suddenly before spilling himself inside me.

Sweaty, exhausted, and boneless, I sink into the mattress with a soft exhale. Propped on his elbows, Grey looks down at me, lazily stroking my jaw with his fingers.

"You're breathtaking," he whispers.

I want to brush off the words, but something about the way his eyes glitter as he speaks them makes me believe he means them.

"You're not terrible, either," I say, still unable to let my guard down completely, even after what we just did.

He smirks and presses a kiss to the tip of my nose before rolling onto his back beside me. I feel better with the bit of distance between us.

The sex was nothing short of amazing, but now that the heat of the moment is over, reality sets in fast, and I'm back to being unsure of what this is. And whether it's safe to want it at all.

"Stay here." He rolls out of bed with a grunt, his movements a bit jerky until he's on his feet.

"I can get whatever it is," I start, but he waves me off with a dark look.

"Don't you dare move," he warns.

I lay back and watch as he disappears into the bathroom. Water runs, and a moment later he reappears with a washcloth. He perches on the edge of the bed and gently nudges my knee aside so he can clean me. His touch is gentle, but even so, when he's done, he looks up at me uncertainly.

"Are you all right?"

My heart softens despite every effort not to let it.

"I'm fine," I tell him, flashing a reassuring smile.

He exhales. "I didn't mean to be so rough…"

I sit up and lean over, pressing a kiss to the side of his mouth. "I asked for it," I whisper, and his lips twitch.

"You did," he agrees.

He gets up and tosses the washcloth in the hamper then returns to bed. This time, he pulls the covers back, and when I try to leave, he grabs me by the waist and yanks me against him.

"Not so fast," he says against my ear, pulling me back against his chest. "I'm not letting you get away that easily."

"We need to change your bandages," I tell him.

"Mm. Tomorrow."

He tucks me in against him and settles in, clearly ready to pass out, and that softening sensation in my chest becomes complete mush. Sex is one thing, though.

Sleeping together is another thing altogether. Despite how adorable and sweet he's being, staying in this room overnight is a terrible fucking idea. I trust Grey with my life, but I'm not naïve enough to think I can trust him with my heart.

I WAKE to sunlight streaming in through windows that are all wrong for the bedroom's layout. Blinking awake quickly, I realize the windows aren't wrong at all, the room is. I'm in Grey's bed—and I'm naked. Grey is nowhere to be seen, but the scent of brewed coffee wafts back from the kitchen. I get up and slip into Grey's closet, snagging a large tee from one of the drawers before making my way toward the scent of fresh caffeine.

Grey looks up from the bowl where he's mixing batter, and I tense as I wait to see whether last night will be acknowledged or forgotten. But the moment he sees me, he sets aside the breakfast makings to wrap his arms around me and pull me into his chest.

"Morning, gorgeous," he murmurs before brushing my mouth with a soft kiss.

"Mm, morning," I say, melting into his touch. Or maybe it's my relief at knowing this is the version of him I'm getting today. Maybe I'm no longer his prisoner after all.

"Sleep well?"

"What little sleep I got was great," I tease.

He smirks. "Complaining?"

"Not at all."

"Good, because I'd hate to have to send you to bed

alone tonight." His words are meant to be a threat, but all I can think is that he plans on continuing what we started last night.

"What? No smartass comeback for that one?" he teases.

"I just...wasn't sure you'd want a repeat performance," I say carefully.

His humor vanishes. In its place is an intensity that makes me squirm out of his grasp. I cover my discomfort by grabbing a mug and pouring myself a cup of coffee.

Behind me, he says, "I want to repeat the performance for as long as you'll let me." I turn back as he adds, "The question is, what do you want, Lexi?"

"What do you mean?"

"I brought you here against your will, and then my father coerced you into marrying me. None of this has been your choice, and I don't want to continue to force you into anything else you don't want."

"You didn't force me into anything," I assure him.

"No, I didn't. You wanted me last night. Even without my wolf's heightened senses, I could scent it, feel it, taste it. But what about tonight and tomorrow and the day after?"

"What about it?" I'm stalling. We both know it.

He steps closer, which only makes my pulse race faster. I grip the mug tightly to keep from dropping it.

"Do you want me, Lexi?" He backs me against the counter and takes the mug from my hands, setting it aside then boxing me in. "Do you want me in your bed?"

"Yes," I whisper.

He traces my bottom lip with his thumb, his brow lifting in a sexy arch. "In your mouth?" he challenges.

I'm already turned on, but at his words, heat slams into me. "Yes."

His thumb releases me, and his hand trails down between my thighs to brush my clit. "In your pussy?"

I swallow hard, rocking forward to meet his touch. "Yes."

He releases me, and my disappointment must show on my face because his mouth quirks. But instead of stroking me again, his palm presses against my chest as he says, "What about in your heart?"

His question is surprisingly serious and carries so much more meaning than the ones that came before it. That was sex. This is... everything.

I lick my lips, hesitating. More than anything, I want to say yes, not because he's turned me on enough that I'll say what he wants, though I have a feeling it's part of the test. I want to say yes because it's true. But I've learned the hard way that, in this world, truth does not set you free.

"I want to," I admit.

He drops his hand and steps back. Something flashes in his eyes. Disappointment or maybe hurt. It's there and gone before I can be sure. It's stupid, but I feel like, for once, I'm the asshole.

Before I can think of something to say to end this awkward moment, he picks up my coffee and pushes it back into my hands.

"Grey," I begin.

He blinks, and his expression is once again smooth and confident, and unaffected. He presses a kiss to my cheek and then goes back to stirring the batter. "I appreciate your honesty, princess. Now, the real question right now is how many pancakes do you want?"

Over breakfast, the awkwardness from earlier is forgotten. Grey is surprisingly good at pancakes though I make sure not to let on how good. He's already way too full of himself.

I reach for a second helping, and his brows lift.

"You have a hollow leg or something?" he teases.

"I'm like a camel," I tease. "Saving it up for later."

He doesn't laugh though. "Lexi, there's no famine to worry about. Not with me."

I shrug like it's no big deal, but inside, my feelings churn because he's just seen right through to the part of me I wasn't offering up for inspection.

When we're finished, I do the dishes while he sips his coffee at the bar. I can feel him watching me, but every time I glance back, he simply winks and grins. He's keeping it light, which makes my guilt return double-time after brushing him off earlier.

"I was wondering if you might help me with something," I say when I'm done cleaning up.

"I thought I already did that last night."

I toss the dishtowel at him, and he catches it with a smirk.

"I mean with my wolf. I need to know why I don't have one. And maybe how to get it back—if that's possible."

I don't mention the fact that I've been wondering about all this since the moment I found out I had shifter blood. Or the fact that I haven't asked him for help before now because I wasn't sure I could trust him with this. But I have a feeling he knows all of that anyway. And it's the most trust I can offer at the moment. I hope he sees that I'm trying to offer more.

He studies me for a moment then nods. "All right, princess. I'll help you find your wolf."

"You will?"

"But you have to do something for me."

I smirk. "I thought I did that last night."

"Oh, believe me, your help last night is much appreciated, but it's not what I want in exchange for this favor."

"Then what—?"

"Let me take you out."

"Like, on a date?"

"Yes. On a date."

"I don't understand."

"Well, it usually consists of dinner and maybe a movie or a walk through the park or—"

"I know what a date is. I just don't get why you want one with me."

"You're my fiancé," he says, and something in me wilts a little.

Of course. We're engaged—and the entire city thinks we're madly in love. Vincenzo won't let us stay locked away in this penthouse. We have to play the part.

"Right. I get it."

He frowns. "Do you? Because I don't just mean—"

"I'll go out with you," I tell him quickly because maybe he hasn't yet realized I would have been commanded to do this eventually by his father, so it's a small price to pay for figuring out why I can't shift.

"All right, princess." His tone is off, but I have no idea

what I've done wrong. I agreed to his terms, so why does he look so irritated?

"Is there something else?"

"Not at all." He sets his mug aside and stands. "We'll go tonight. I'll make sure the paparazzi are expecting us."

27

GREY

She isn't ready to trust me yet, and it's no one's fault but my own. I kidnapped her and threw her into a world intent on using or destroying her, so what did I expect when I finally realized I was in love with her? Fuck. Even admitting it to myself in my head still feels surreal. I have no idea when I knew. Sometime last night while I was fucking her, it hit me. This wasn't about fucking. This was about her. And the moment I understood it, my wolf came roaring back. I haven't told her that part. I haven't even used it to help me heal yet. Hell, having him back so soon shouldn't be possible after what my father did. The only thing that makes sense is Lexi.

She's my mate.

Otherwise, being with her last night shouldn't have been able to break my father's alpha order over me. It's the only explanation for wanting to bite her and claim her right there on my mattress as she came for me.

Now, she refuses to trust me, and that's on no one else but me.

But, fuck, it's infuriating.

Before I can take my anger out on her, I stalk back to my room and close the door, sealing her off from my bad mood. Two days ago, leaving her alone in the apartment wouldn't have been an option, but now, I don't worry. She might not trust me with her heart, but I know she understands I'll keep her safe from the dangers that await her beyond these walls.

After a shower and fresh clothes, I step onto my balcony and call Dutch.

It's barely ten in the morning and already warm enough to be uncomfortable, but I need the privacy.

Dutch answers sleepily. "Yeah?"

"You still sleeping?"

"Not anymore, asshole."

"I need advice."

"Hang on." There's a pause and then, "Okay, I just had to check out the window to see if we had an ice storm last night."

"What the fuck are you talking about?"

"If you want advice from me, it can only mean hell has officially frozen over."

"Fuck off," I say, but he ignores me, laughing at his own joke. "Are you done?"

"Okay—okay, what's up?"

"Lexi and I slept together."

"Fucking finally," he declares. "How was she?"

A growl rips from my throat.

"Whoa, tiger. Forget I asked. Why the hell do you need sex advice from me, anyway? A little late in the game for the birds and the bees talk, isn't it?"

I grip the phone tight, trying to keep from cussing him out. If I do that, he'll hang up, and I won't have any answers.

"It's not about sex. That part's… good."

"Just good—?"

"Dutch," I snap.

"Okayyy. Get to the point. I need to piss."

"I want her to trust me with more than just sex."

He's quiet so long that I wonder if he hung up.

"Dutch?"

"I'm trying not to make a big deal about this. Give me a second."

I sigh. "By saying that, you are making a big deal about it."

"Bro, you're in love with her. How is that not a big deal?"

"I'm…" I can't bring myself to argue even if hearing it out loud terrifies me. "Yeah, I am."

"Does this mean… is she your… but no, your wolf isn't even accessible right now."

"He's back," I say quietly.

"That was fast. The old man took mercy on you?"

"No. She brought it back."

"No shit. The only way that's possible is if she's your—"

"Mate," I finish for him, unable to keep the grim tone out of my voice.

"Dude, that's—"

"Don't say it's great," I warn. "It's fucking terrible, all things considered. But I'm not losing this war, and I'm not losing her either. So, I need you to help me make her trust me, or else she'll end up doing something stupid, and I'll end up getting us all killed over it."

I brace myself, fully expecting him to make some smart-ass joke, but he gets serious as he says, "This is going to piss you off, but the fact is she shouldn't trust you. You fucking kidnapped her ass and locked her in a tower. She should hate you."

I groan. "I know. That's why I need your advice."

"Look, you've had all the power all along, and she's had none."

"I can't go back and change what happened."

"You don't have to. Just let her have some control, bro. She needs to feel free."

"Are you about to give me one of those 'if you love someone set them free' cliches?"

"Fuck no. That's stupid. If you love her, you have to show her. And in this case, that means giving her back what you took from her in the first place."

"Control. Freedom," I repeat, hating that he's right.

"Exactly."

"How do I do that?"

He snorts. "That's for you to figure out."

"I thought you were giving me advice."

"I just did. Look, I can't do all the work, boss. This part's on you."

Before I can argue, he disconnects but not before I hear the distinct sound of him peeing.

Classy.

An hour later, I've managed to secure us a reservation at Mannino's. It's one of the most sought-after restaurants in the city, but it's also discreet. I lied about the paparazzi and am doing my best to coordinate an evening where we can be out together and still have our privacy.

Freedom, I remind myself.

But I know it's not enough.

With the table booked, I call Mia next.

"What's up?" she answers, breathing heavily.

"Where are you?"

"On a treadmill, nosy. What's up?"

I blow out a breath, letting my worry go with it. Clearly, I'm on edge and need to relax. "I need a favor."

"Shoot."

"Lexi needs an outfit for tonight. Can you take her shopping?"

"Tonight? Did Vincenzo add something else to the calendar?"

"No." I hesitate. "I'm taking her out."

"Let me guess, Vincenzo's sending paparazzi to accidentally discover you being in love?"

"My father isn't part of this."

"Oh." Her surprise and ensuing silence speak volumes. But I know Mia, and she's not going to let this go. Right on time, she says, "You want to explain to me why you've been completely against love for the better part of your entire life, and the moment you meet the least available woman, you immediately change your mind?"

"I'd rather not explain anything," I say.

"Grey Diavolo. She's literally the most off-limits woman you could have chosen."

"I'm aware."

"Your father will kill you both."

"I'm aware of that too."

She sighs and then swears in Italian, something she's done since seventh grade when she took a full year of the language and only learned the bad words.

"Will you take her?" I ask, hoping the worst is over with her.

Then again, I have no doubt she's going to spread this news to the others, and it'll only get worse once Razor and Ramsey hear about this.

"Of course," Mia says. "I'll send a car in an hour."

"Thanks."

"Don't thank me; just owe me one." Her tone is smug, and I shake my head. I should have known this wouldn't be a freebie.

"Fine," I tell her. "See you in an hour."

After ending the call, I go in search of Lexi and find her curled up on the couch, watching a movie I've never seen before.

"What are you watching?" I ask, stopping beside the couch rather than sitting on it.

Dutch's words echo from earlier. I need to give her the control, which probably means giving her space too.

When she doesn't answer, I look over to find her staring at me with clear judgment in her expression.

"What?" I ask.

"It's Furious Seven." At my blank look, she adds, "Tell me you've seen the Fast and Furious movies."

I shrug. "I don't really watch TV."

"Wow, I finally feel sorry for you."

A smile tugs at the corner of my mouth. I sit on the armrest, still keeping space between us. She hits the pause button on the remote, which she apparently figured out how to use while I was gone.

"What happened to Claire?" she asks.

I blink, trying to understand where the question came from. "Mia cleaned her up and took her home."

"So she's safe," Lexi says.

"Of course."

She bites her lip, and I wait, but she doesn't ask anything else. Part of me wants to push it, but I remind myself of the bigger picture and focus on my plan.

"Our dinner reservation is set for eight," I tell her.

"Oh." She blinks as if just remembering our conversation. "Okay, is it fancy?"

"It's black tie," I say.

She starts to rise. "I don't know if I have anything else in the clothes you bought me, but I'll check the wardrobe."

"Actually, I was thinking you could pick out your own outfit."

She stops and looks at me warily, and I realize how little control she really has—and how right Dutch is about offering her some.

"Exactly how would I do that? From an app on your phone?"

"I was thinking you could shop for it yourself. Mia's sending a car for you in an hour."

Something flickers in her eyes. Disappointment? There's a wall up between us after our conversation earlier, and I can't read her. My chest tightens as I wait for her to give me some sort of response. If she doesn't want to spend time with Mia—

"You trust her to babysit me instead of doing it your-self?" she asks.

I frown. "It's not about babysitting. I just thought you might like the company of another woman. You're welcome to go alone if you prefer."

"Alone," she repeats skeptically.

"I'd send security, of course, but that's for your safety. My driver will take you anywhere you want to go."

She stares at me, and I get the distinct impression it's not enough. But it's all I can offer her. For now.

"I'll go with Mia," she says eventually.

I nod, trying to hide my relief. "Just tell them to put your purchases on my account. I'll take care of whatever it is you pick out."

I rise and start back to my bedroom, already thinking of a few more calls I can make to ensure this day goes smoothly for her.

"Grey."

The sound of her voice stops me. I look back and find her watching me from across the living room. Something flashes in her gorgeous eyes.

"Yes?"

"Have you ever seen Pretty Woman?"

"No."

She looks relieved. "Good."

28

LEXI

*A*fter showering and changing into a pair of jeans and a cropped tee, I sit alone and pretend to watch the movie I've chosen. It's packed full of high-speed car maneuvers and a cast who will do anything to protect the people they care about. The Fast and Furious movies are favorites I'll watch again and again. Today, I'm too distracted to appreciate it. Grey's dinner invitation did weird things to my insides—right up until he reminded me this is all part of our game.

I hate how much it hurts to know he's only taking me out so that the paparazzi can feed our fake love story to the unsuspecting residents of Indigo Hills. Mostly, I hate how much I already care for a guy who clearly doesn't care for me beyond being a means to an end. We might not be on opposite sides anymore, but that doesn't mean we're friends.

All morning, I've been replaying the last few days with him, trying to figure out who he really is when he doesn't think anyone's looking. It made me think of Claire and how he handed her off to Mia like he'd rescued girls like her before. But I can't assume anything. Even if he does things like cuddle and cook me pancakes. Because when morning comes, reality has a way of crashing back down around us—a fact he reminded me of when he planned this dinner around the paparazzi.

By the time Mia's car arrives, I've decided two can play this game of politics and pretend. Tonight, I'll show up to that dinner looking like the arm candy he's asked for. And if he tries taking me back to bed again, I'll make sure he knows that, if he wanted dessert, he should have ordered it at the restaurant.

At the elevator, Grey stops me and pushes a small black box into my hands.

"What's this?" I ask, a lump forming in my stomach as I stare down at the velvet jewelry box.

"Open it."

I do, hating that my hands shake a little as I lift the lid. The diamond ring nestled inside is bigger than any I've ever seen and rips a small gasp from my lips.

"Do you like it?"

"It's way too much," I say, my stomach full of butterflies that clearly don't understand the situation at all.

It's fake, I remind myself. Just like this relationship. So why do I care so much that he thought to buy me a ring?

"It's exactly what they'll expect for the Giovanni princess."

"Right." I shake off the feelings threatening to make me look like a fool and wait while he plucks the ring from the box and slides it onto my finger. It's a perfect fit—which means absolutely nothing.

I flash him a tight smile. "Good guess on the size."

He doesn't respond to that. Instead, he pulls out a phone and presses it into my hand. "My number's programmed in case you need anything. When you're finished, Mia will deliver you here to get dressed, and then I'll send a car for you at seven-thirty."

"You won't be here when I get back?"

"I have some things to take care of."

I wait, but he doesn't elaborate, which is another reminder that I'm not his friend. Nor am I a trusted ally as he claims.

"Fine." I take the phone and shove it into my bag then step into the elevator. Turning around to face him, I press the button and note the deep frown he's wearing. But I don't meet his eyes before the door closes and he's gone.

Outside, a black sedan is parked at the curb. A male driver with graying hair smiles at me as I approach.

"Miss Giovanni." He holds open the back passenger door for me to slide inside.

Mia's already seated in the backseat.

"Hey." She takes one look at me and immediately zeroes in on the diamond. Not that you can miss it. The thing's like a giant disco ball sitting on my finger. Or a sun with its own solar system. "Whoa. He went all out."

"I guess." I slide my hand away, tucking it beneath the fabric of my pants.

Her eyes narrow as we pull away from the curb. "Trouble in paradise already?"

I cut her a look. "What paradise?"

"Touché," she says with a wry smile. "Indigo Hills is no

241

destination retreat, I'll give you that, but you haven't seen our shopping district yet, either."

"I'm not much of a shopper," I admit.

She stares at me with a look of pure horror. "What blasphemy is this?"

I shake my head. "I guess it's just not my thing."

She pats my arm like she's trying to comfort me. "Don't worry, there's still time to fix you."

I can't help but laugh.

Ten minutes later, we're pulling up to the curb in front of a plaza that hosts several high-end boutiques whose names I can hardly pronounce. The area between them all is paved with a fountain in the center that is surrounded by benches and landscaped plants.

"Come on," Mia says. "We'll start with Les Haut and go from there."

The moment we're out of the car, she's full steam ahead, leading me across the plaza like a woman on a mission.

For the next hour, I'm whisked into and out of at least six different shops, each one more expensive than the last. Mia's version of shopping is like nothing I've ever experienced before. In the past, I'd always been very aware of what little money I have to spend and only chose places with cheap prices or huge sales. Since money was always limited, I never shopped in more than a couple of stores at a time. But I quickly learn that with Mia, shopping is a sport, and it's all about endurance.

Eventually, I must look exhausted enough for her to show me mercy, and we end up in a café eating Greek salads and sipping white wine.

"My feet are killing me," I groan.

"But they're going to look fantastic," she points out.

"True," I admit.

The black strappy heels she paired with the dress I chose at our last stop make a stunning combination. Even I can admit I look hot.

"Now we just have to figure out your hair," she says. "I can call in a favor at my salon. Alejandro would love to get his hands on your head and do a chop—"

"Hold it right there. I am not chopping anything."

"Okay, okay." She picks up her wine. "A blow-out then."

"I guess I could try that," I concede.

She stares at me. "Try it? As in, you've never had one?"

I shrug. "Other than my friend Violet dressing me up for work, no."

Her shock melts into interest. "You really are nothing like the pampered princess they say, are you?"

I snort. "Pampered is not a word you would use if you saw my life."

"What was it like?" she asks.

I stare at her in surprise. "You really want to know?"

"Of course. Why wouldn't I?"

"No one else has asked me that yet."

Her eyes narrow. "Not even Grey?"

"No."

She mumbles something in a language I don't understand.

"What?"

"Nothing. You were saying…"

"Well, I live in a pay-per-week efficiency—"

"Like a hotel?"

"Motel," I correct, smiling wryly at the small shudder

she gives. "It's not fancy, but it's all mine, and that's a step up from the group home where I was before."

Or my car before that.

"What sort of group home?"

"It's a boarding house for orphans who've aged out of foster care and can't rely on the state to pay for their housing anymore."

"Sounds nice."

I blink at her, taking a second to realize she's being serious. "It's not, trust me."

"And you worked at a club?" she asks, clearly not wanting to press further about my living conditions, which is fine with me. I feel zero shame for my past or for living where I did because, at the end of the day, I did it all on my own, and that's something I'm proud of. However, one look at Mia's world and I know there's nothing I can say that will make her understand.

At her question, though, I pick up my wine and smile teasingly. "You can say it, Mia. A *strip* club."

"Okay, I deserved that one." She props her chin on her hand and leans in. "What is it like? Dancing for strangers?"

I lean in too. "Want to find out?" Her eyes widen, and I laugh. "Just say the word, and I can get you in. Shady would love you."

"Is that your boss?"

"Yeah, he owns the place and handpicks all the girls. He'd love a true redhead on his stage."

"Maybe someday." She sits back, considering, which kind of surprises me, though the more I learn about her, the more I realize Mia isn't just the shallow, rich girl. There's a wild woman beneath her money and polish. "For now, I'll stick to getting my kicks from shopping with you."

"You say that like you don't get any thrills out of your life already."

"Risking my life to work against the alpha I've pledged my undying loyalty to is not exactly the thrill I'm looking for."

"What would happen if he found out we're working against him?" I ask.

"He'd kill us," she says, her tone so matter-of-fact that I flinch. "But the idea of him running this city is enough to make me risk it. That and Grey."

For some stupid reason, jealousy flares inside me. "You care about him that much?" I ask, hating that I'm bothered by it.

"I believe in him," she says and then takes one look at me and adds, "Relax. I have zero interest in him that way. He's not my type."

"I didn't—"

"Oh, honey, your feelings are written all over your face. But don't worry; it just means no one's going to doubt this engagement or the two of you together." She reaches across the table and pats my hand. "I'm happy he found someone, Lexi. And I'm happy it's you."

I don't bother to tell her my feelings for Grey aren't mutual. Nor do I point out that, even if it were real, the only way we get to be together is if we go to war against our own families first. None of that should make any of us *happy*.

"What was it like—growing up together?" I can't help but ask.

She looks thoughtful. "Hard. Demanding. Cold. We all had expectations from our families, and since our parents were all generals, we were thrown together a lot. Forgotten together a lot too. For a while, it was just me, Dutch, and Grey. Then, Ramsey's dad got promoted, so he got stuck with us during meetings and outings. Razor came last, and he was already a package deal with Crow—not that we wouldn't have taken him on his own."

"Grey said they have the same dad, but they're not fully brothers?"

"They are brothers," she says, eyes flashing with irritation. She takes a breath and then, more calmly, explains, "Alvaro, Razor's father, had an affair with Crow's mom about a year after Razor was born."

"So, Crow having a different mom makes him an outcast?"

"Worse. Crow's mom wasn't a general's wife, and that makes both of them an outcast. Alvaro and the other generals refuse to recognize him as an heir and basically just ignore him whenever they see him."

"An heir to what?"

She cocks her head. "Is Grey really not telling you how our basic hierarchy works? I thought you two made peace."

My face heats as I say, "We've been busy doing ... other things."

"Ah."

Her smile suggests she's not even surprised, which only makes me want to ask how the hell she knew before I did that Grey wanted me—or what else she knows that I don't. Instead, I clear my throat and force my attention back to the conversation at hand. "You were saying? About Crow not being an heir?"

"Right. It's a stupid scandal that shouldn't even matter in this millennium, but here we are. Being a general is an inherited title in our pack, which means someday, Ramsey, Dutch, Razor, and I will all become one."

"But not Crow."

"Not under the current leadership."

My heart aches for what it must have meant to be rejected by his own family.

"I know how it feels," I say quietly.

Mia reaches across the table and squeezes my hand then releases it quickly. "You're one of us now, just like he is."

I smile at her, feeling a stirring of friendship that I sincerely hope I can trust. "Thanks."

After lunch, we get our nails done, followed by my hair, which thankfully involves zero cutting or chopping. Alejandro *oohs* and *ahhs* over my hair and skin tone until Mia takes mercy on me and gets me out of there.

We're just leaving the salon when I nearly run into someone.

"Oh, sorry." I step back quickly and look up to find a familiar golden boy smiling down at me.

"No apology necessary. It's my lucky day to run into such a beautiful woman—even if she's done it literally."

"Hello, Ramsey."

"Ram, what are you doing here?" Mia asks.

"I had an errand out this way, so Grey asked me to look in on you two. How's the shopping going?"

"Great," Mia tells him.

He eyes us, confused. "But you don't have any bags."

Mia rolls her eyes. "Everything's being delivered to the apartment. Why would we carry it ourselves?"

He meets my eyes, smiling. "Indeed. In that case, do you need a lift home to get dressed?"

"Oh." I check the time, realizing it's getting late already. "Sure, but I think Mia was going to…"

He turns to Mia. "I have to run over to pick something up for Grey anyway. It's no trouble."

Mia shrugs. "Sure. Saves me a trip."

"You sure?" I ask.

"Totally." She reaches over and kisses my cheek. "Knock him dead tonight, girl," she whispers in my ear.

I grin back at her. "That's the plan."

She waves and traipses off toward a jewelry store, leaving me alone with Ramsey.

"Shall we?" he asks, and I fall into step beside him.

I expect him to have his own car and driver like the others, but he leads me into the parking garage and over to a sportscar I've only ever read about in auto magazines.

I stop when he pulls open the passenger door for me.

"What's wrong?" he asks.

"Is this the new Lykan Hypersport?" I ask, staring at the sleek black paint job with silver accents.

"Yeah, you know cars?"

"Only the fast ones," I murmur, lightly running a hand over the hood before sliding inside. The white leather bucket seats are soft as butter beneath my skin. After buckling, I stare at the dashboard, which is lit up like a gaming console.

Ramsey climbs in beside me and starts the engine with the press of a button. The purr is music to my ears.

"This is yours?" I ask him.

"Birthday present," he says as casually as if he'd been gifted a pair of socks.

"This is one of the most expensive cars on the market," I say. "And the fastest. Off the line, it beat out every single one of its competitors."

"Then I guess it better be fucking fast, huh?" He winks and backs out of the space, revving a little before pulling quickly into traffic. "So, how do you know so much about Panthers?"

"Sometimes, on the weekend, I go to the magazine aisle and just read."

He glances at me and his expression shifts. "You're serious. Why?"

"I like cars, and I didn't have anything better to do."

Or any money.

"You're an interesting person, Lexi Giovanni."

"Lexi Ryall," I correct automatically before realizing he's right.

Thankfully, he doesn't argue.

Traffic makes opening up the engine impossible, but I still enjoy the drive and the car. In fact, I'm so distracted by it that it takes me a while to realize we're not headed back toward Grey's apartment.

"I think we're going the wrong way," I say when I begin to recognize the high rises of the business district.

"Nah, just a shortcut." Ramsey doesn't look over.

I feel a strange prickle of unease run down my spine. "What did you say you were doing at the plaza?" I ask.

"Just running an errand." He glances over, his expression strangely blank. "What a coincidence, right?"

"Right," I echo, my pulse beginning to speed up as we make another turn that takes us farther away from the apartment. Pulling my phone out of my bag, I pull up Grey's programmed number, still trying to appear casual. "I'm just going to call Grey and let him know."

Ramsey snatches the phone from my hand before I can hit the button.

I stare at him, fear replacing suspicion. "What are you—"

"No calls," he says in a voice I've never heard him use before.

"Ramsey, what's going on? Where are you taking me?"

His expression is tight as he grips the wheel. "Look, I'm sorry, okay?"

But he doesn't sound sorry, only desperate.

"For what?" I press. "What's going on?"

We pull to a sudden stop, and I look over just as Ramsey says, "He only wants to talk to you; he swore to me."

I don't have to ask who Ramsey is referring to. Outside my window, I spot a familiar alley. It's long and narrow, running the length of the block full of buildings, each one tall enough to scrape the sky except for a squat, two-story restaurant smack in the middle of the block. There's no sign back here, but I remember escaping through this very alley just a couple of days ago.

Dead ahead is Altobello's.

"Ramsey, what the hell are you doing?" I ask, heart thudding now.

His voice is grim as he says, "Get out of the car."

"Ramsey," I try again.

He squeezes his eyes shut like he's in pain. "I didn't have a choice, all right?"

"Did they threaten you? Grey can protect you. He can—"

"Get out of the fucking car!"

29

LEXI

Fully aware of just how screwed I am, I do what Ramsey says and get out of the car. He doesn't follow like I expect him to, though, and the moment I realize I'm alone—that idiot thought I was stupid enough to think I'd just walk willingly down this alley and into that back door—I run. My shoes are a hindrance, so I kick them off, sprinting past pedestrians as I flee blindly toward the safety of the main road. As if safety exists anywhere in this city. My sense of direction is immediately lost, but I keep going, knowing I need to get as far from here as I possibly can before—

A hand grabs me from behind, lifting me clear off my feet.

I scream, kicking wildly against the solid wall of muscle currently holding me hostage in an iron grip. The pressure around my ribs is so tight it's hard to breathe, but I manage another scream anyway. A hand clamps over my mouth, and I catch the scent of a musky cologne, the scent so strong he might as well have bathed in the stuff.

Dom.

I'd know his version of overdone luxury anywhere.

"Shut up, and stop fighting," he orders, his irritated voice in my ear confirming it's him.

With a hand over my mouth and another around my waist, he holds my back against his chest as he carries me down the street toward the front of the restaurant. The front doors loom like the gates of Hell, and I have the distinct feeling that, if I go through them, I'll never come out again.

Fear grips me then.

Redoubling my efforts, I manage to land a kick that makes Dom grunt, but it's not enough to loosen his hold. Around me, pedestrians stare as they pass, but no one stops him or even comments on the kidnapping taking place right before their eyes.

For some reason, this is the moment I realize how different Indigo Hills really is from the rest of the world. It's not about wolf shifters or anything supernatural; it's this—regular citizens witnessing an obvious crime and doing nothing to stop it.

This city is a killer, and I've just become its next victim.

Despite my thrashing, Dom carries me right through the front doors of Altobello's and promptly releases me. I fall into a heap on the floor, grunting with the impact. Ignoring the pain of the hard floor against my knees and elbows, I climb quickly to my feet and assess my surroundings. Three security guards already block the door behind me. Their expressions are grim and unyielding though they don't bother meeting my eyes.

Like I'm not even here.

Like I never even existed.

Will anyone miss me when I'm dead?

Mia? Violet? Grey?

His name makes my eyes burn with hot tears, but I refuse to give in to them. Blinking away the moisture, I note the bartender from the other day back at his post. Bobby something or other. He looks over at me, and I flash him my middle finger. He chuckles and goes back to polishing glasses.

"Classy," Dom says.

I recover and glare at him. "Fuck you."

He stalks up to me so quickly that I shrink away from him. But he only leans in closer until I can smell his stale breath as he says, "You play your cards right, princess, you might just get your wish someday."

He flashes me a parting wink, and it takes every ounce of my self-control not to chase him down and claw his eyes out with my freshly painted nails. Then again, if I'm about to die anyway, why hold myself back?

The back door swings open, and Franco steps out. Three more men enter behind him and fan out into the space. They all wear the same slacks and button-downs as the guards at the front door. I'm starting to realize "business killer casual" is a specific look in Indigo Hills. Like every bodyguard in the city shops at the same store or something.

"Boss, she's here," Dom says.

"No shit, Sherlock. I can see her standing there." Franco frowns as he pauses in front of Dom. "What the hell happened to you?"

Dom dabs at his cheek, and I feel a sense of satisfaction

at the blood that stains his fingers when he pulls his hand away. He looks over, glaring at me as he realizes I actually injured him.

"Classy," I toss back at him.

His eyes narrow, and he starts toward me, but Franco stops him. Instead, the old man himself strides over to where I stand, disheveled and terrified, though I'm hoping he doesn't notice the latter.

"You wanted to see me so badly the other day," he taunts. "Now, you've suddenly changed your mind?"

"I've re-evaluated."

He smiles smugly. "So have I."

At the back, another guard pushes through the doorway from the kitchen. He glances around the room then settles on Franco.

"Found him in the alley outside," he says.

Then he moves aside to reveal a familiar face.

Ramsey.

"Dismissed," Franco tells the guard.

The man retreats into the kitchen, leaving Ramsey standing before us. Rage builds inside me all over again at seeing him in the same room with Franco and Dom. He's the enemy now, and I want nothing more to do with him except to pay him back for his betrayal.

"You're not worried your people will see you here?" Franco asks him.

"Of course I am. But your guy did a snatch-and-grab on the street before I even pulled away. I can't be seen driving off and leaving her ass here."

"Take a seat and shut your mouth then." Franco waves

him off toward the bar, and I'm surprised to watch as Ramsey does as he's ordered.

Franco turns back to me. "Now, about that re-evaluation."

"Whatever you're going to do to me, it won't matter." I muster all the bravery I can as he cocks his head, studying me with an expression that says he knows I'm full of shit.

"And why is that?"

"Because the Diavolo family doesn't care what happens to me, so there's no point in trying to use me against them."

"Is that what you think?"

I frown. "It's the truth."

"Regardless of what you believe, I called you here for a purpose."

A purpose.

Was death a purpose?

I wasn't sure, but I also wasn't ready to let my guard down.

"I don't give a shit about your purpose."

"You will," he says in a voice that makes me shudder.

"There's nothing you can ask of me that I'll agree to."

He ignores my words and simply says, "Find out what Diavolo is planning, and report back to me."

"Vincenzo? I already told you, he's—"

"Not Vincenzo. The son."

My gaze flicks to Ramsey, and dread punches me in the gut. "You told him?"

Ramsey's expression crumples into silent anguish, but I feel zero empathy for whatever has him twisted up just now. All I can do is stare at him in horror and disgust.

"You fucking ratted on your best friend?" I demand.

"You don't understand," Ramsey says, but I cut him off and look back at Franco.

"You want me to spy for you?" I say in disbelief. "After abandoning and rejecting me? Are you serious?"

"I am."

"Go to hell."

Franco moves surprisingly fast for an old man. His hand shoots out, cracking across my cheek with enough force to make me stumble sideways. Fiery pain blooms across my skin, and my eyes water.

"You will do as I tell you, girl." Franco's voice is clipped with barely controlled anger.

Blinking furiously, I cup my cheek with my hand and focus on breathing. Now that I know what he really wants, I can't help but think being dumped into a vat of acid would have been so much easier.

"Or what?" I challenge, squaring my shoulders and meeting his gaze like I'm not a completely terrified mess.

"Or the next miserable fuck I snatch off the street will be your precious fiancé."

"I don't care about Grey."

"Bullshit," he snorts, and I realize he's seen right through me. Mia was right; I suck at lying. "Though, if you want to test me, be my guest. His death will be on you, and so will the long hours of torture that come before it. But if you don't care...by all means, refuse me. The choice is yours, Granddaughter."

The last word drips with sarcasm, and I decide right here that I hate him. There is absolutely no bond or debt owed to this man for being my blood. He's evil and deserves what he gets.

After a beat of silence, I hear, "Lexi."

My head whips toward Ramsey where he sends me a pleading look. Before I can tell him to go fuck himself, Franco grabs my chin and yanks me back to face him.

"Do we have a deal?" he snaps.

I hesitate, my heart pounding so hard I wonder how it doesn't bruise my ribs. "What do you want me to find out?"

30

GREY

*T*he maître d' shoots me another glance, eliciting a growl from me. With one hand, I grip the half-full Old Fashioned I've already drained twice. With the other, I hold my phone, doing my best not to crush it in my hands as I stare at the unanswered texts I've sent to Lexi.

She's late.

Ramsey texted me an hour ago and said Lexi was upset after shopping and he'd wait to make sure she got out of the apartment okay. He's checked in with me since, buying more time, but she refuses to answer me.

Part of me wants to call Mia and demand to know what she said to make Lexi so upset. But then I remember none of this is Mia's fault. It's mine.

I've been an asshole.

I kidnapped her, for fuck's sake. Dragged her to a foreign city and straight into a feud that could very well get her killed. And now, I want her to choose me like some lovesick fucking fool. One day of shopping and the illusion of freedom will not change what I am to her.

The maître d' looks over again and I squeeze the glass, imagining it's his head. His judgment is written clearly over his sympathetic features. He already believes I've been stood up, and he feels sorry.

Pity is one thing I will not allow.

Lexi has to come. She just has to—

My phone rings, cutting off my spiraling thoughts. Hope leaps into my throat, but instead of Lexi's burner phone number on my Caller ID, it's my father.

Fuck.

He's the last person I want to speak to now.

But since I know he has eyes and ears even here in this restaurant, I answer it.

"Hello, Father."

"What are you doing?" he demands, and I set the glass down because, this time, I already know I'll squeeze it hard enough to shatter it.

"Having dinner."

"Where the hell is the girl?"

I frown, purposely keeping my eyes averted even though all I want to do is scan the faces of the other diners. Someone here is informing to him about me, and I want to know who.

"She's coming."

"Coming? What the fuck? You were supposed to keep her leashed," he says, voice rising, probably right along with his blood pressure. "To never take your eyes off her. Where the hell is she?"

"She's secure," I say, my voice tightening as his volume rises.

"Unless she's under the table sucking you off, I beg to differ."

Rage boils inside me, and I grip the tablecloth if only to have something grounding me to this Earth—and to the reasons why I shouldn't rip his tongue out.

"Don't talk about her that way." The words rip from my mouth, and the moment I say them, I wish I could take them back.

"You care about her."

It's not a question, but I can't let it go. "No," I lie. "You're just being a dick."

"What does she mean to you, son? More than whore, clearly." He pauses, but I refuse to dignify any of this with a response. "Do you actually *want* to marry her?"

I expect anger or even disappointment, so his quiet curiosity puts me on edge. "That's ridiculous. I just met her."

"True, but mates don't need time, only recognition."

"She has no wolf," I remind him. "There's no mate to recognize."

"She has a wolf," he says in a voice that sends a trickle of unease down my spine.

"What do you know about her wolf?" I demand.

"Not enough yet," he says. "But I will soon."

I don't know what that means, but my mind is already working a mile a minute to think of a way to find out.

"And when I do," he goes on, "She'll be ours to control forever."

Not ours.

Mine.

I start to argue but then shut my mouth again before I can make things worse. He must take my silence as agreement because he clears his throat and says, "I'll be in touch. Enjoy your dinner."

The moment we hang up, I lift my hand and signal for another drink. At the same time, I dial Dutch to fill him in and ask him to look into whatever my father's hiding about Lexi's wolf. Whatever it is, it can't be good for her. I don't need details to know Vincenzo is only out for himself in the end because that's the only person in the world he's ever looked out for.

I used to be that way. Only looking out for myself too. Hell, it's why my plan failed five years ago and why I left when it did. But now, I have someone else's fate to think about. Lexi's future is in my hands—and I've never felt less capable of saving anyone in my entire fucking life.

Find out what happens next in Deadly Wolf Bite!

Want more from this world?
Check out The Lone Wolf Pack series & The Black Moon
Pack series for interconnected shifter romance stories and
see which characters from Dark Wolf Soul make an
appearance.

Find out more including series reading order at https://
www.heatherhildenbrand.com/series-reading-order.

ABOUT THE AUTHOR

Heather Hildenbrand lives in coastal Virginia where she writes paranormal and urban fantasy romance with lots of kissing & killing. Her most frequent hobbies are truck camping with her goldendoodle, talking to her plants, and avoiding killer slugs.

You can find out more about Heather and her books at www.heatherhildenbrand.com.

Or find her here:

Facebook
Facebook reader group
Instagram
Subscribe to her Newsletter & get a free book!
TikTok
Patreon

Made in the USA
Middletown, DE
08 September 2023